I0746617

BRANCHES OF BETRAYAL

MODERN GODDESS SERIES BOOK TWO

SARAH JAMES

PRAISE

FOR THE MODERN GODDESS SERIES

"Jaw, meet floor. The madness. The passion. The chaos. This entire book left me reeling and wanting Hadina to burn my world down around me." —Dahlia Reign, author of the *Agostino Crime Family* series

"It's everything we love about Hades x Persephone retellings, but with a delicious sapphic twist!" —@ericasbookshelf, bookish content creator

"A deliciously raw and addictive sapphic mafia romance. Sarah James is an author to watch!" —Jessica S. Taylor, author of the *Seas of Caladhan* duology

"This book was a surprising breath of fresh air. The perfect introduction to dark sapphic romance, with a side of mafia. The Hades and Persephone retelling we deserve." —@corvinascloud, book reviewer

"From book one, I was hooked! Peyton and Hadina are a breath of fresh air in this cartel-esque series. I waited with bated breath for book two and I was not disappointed. I can't wait to read more from Sarah James in the future!"

—V. Domino, author of *An Acapulco Affair* & *The Lies Duet*

BRANCHES OF BETRAYAL | Sarah James

First Edition | Publication Date: September 15, 2024

Paperback ISBN: 978-1-7384105-3-8

Hardcover ISBN: 978-1-7384105-4-5

Ebook ASIN: B0CW1FS2V3

Cover design by V. Domino @3Crows.Author.Services

Formatting by V. Domino @3Crows.Author.Services

SARAH JAMES

Author Note

Branches of Betrayal is the second book in a dark contemporary romance series, loosely inspired by Greek mythology. Branches of Betrayal takes inspiration from the Hades and Persephone myth, though it is definitely *not* a retelling.

Branches of Betrayal also features a queer, Latinx female main character. Coming to the decision to make a main character in the book Mexican-American was not one that I came to lightly. As a White author, I know that I am not the voice of Latinx people. However, I firmly believe that there is a lack of representation in fiction and I strive to help change this.

My aim is not to tell the story of Latinx people, but rather portray them as accurately as possible in my works so that they feel represented in literature. If there is anything at all that you feel is inappropriate, inaccurate or needs to be changed, please do not hesitate to contact me. You can reach me at authorsarahj@gmail.com and I will apply all necessary changes.

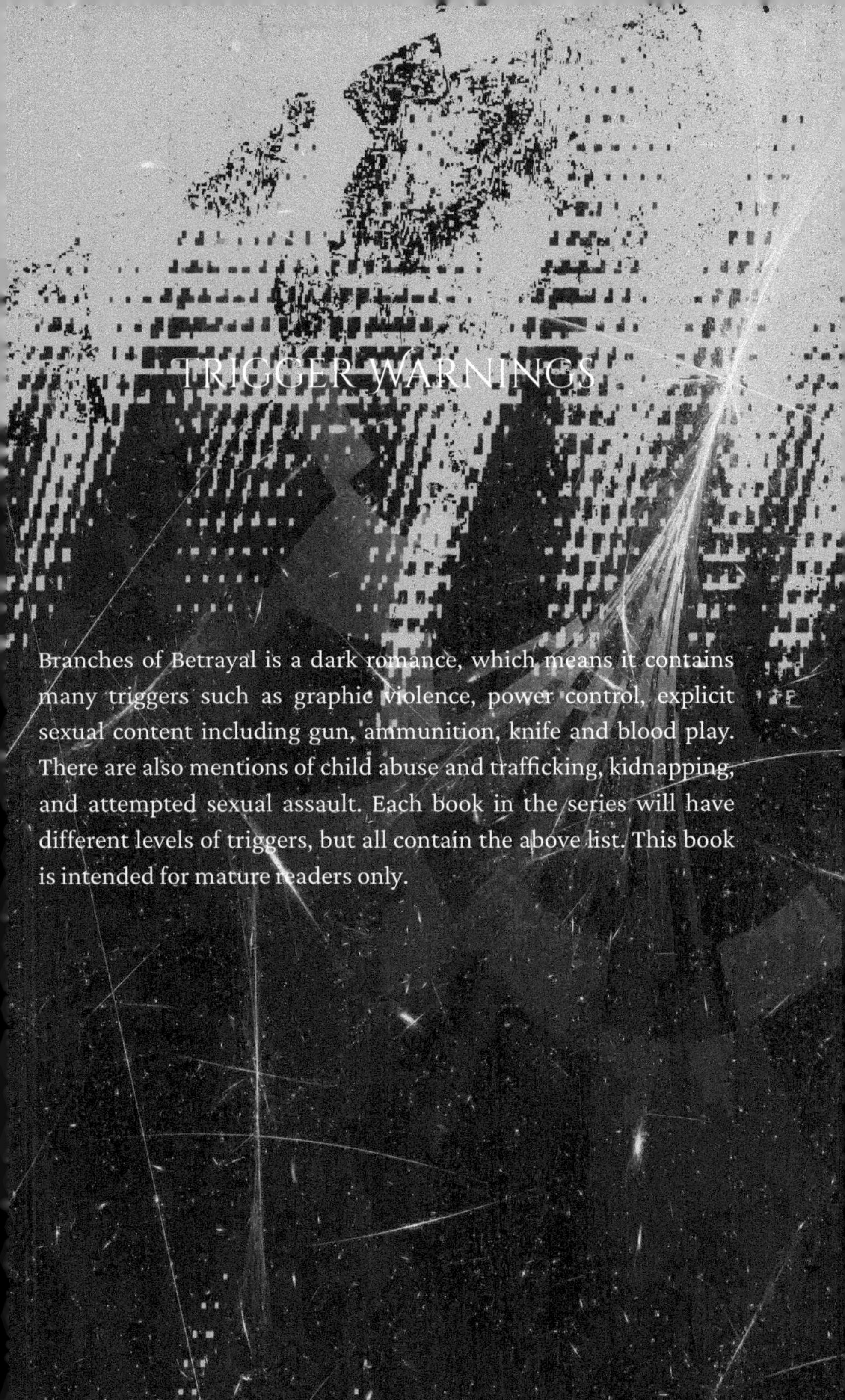

TRIGGER WARNINGS

Branches of Betrayal is a dark romance, which means it contains many triggers such as graphic violence, power control, explicit sexual content including gun, ammunition, knife and blood play. There are also mentions of child abuse and trafficking, kidnapping, and attempted sexual assault. Each book in the series will have different levels of triggers, but all contain the above list. This book is intended for mature readers only.

Dedicated to those who fight for love, even when it hurts.

Adis & Co.
ATTORNEY LAW

PLAYLIST

Efflorescence – Far & Beyond
By Your Side – Marissa
Colors – Elvis Drew
Wallows – Tommy Docherty
I Want It All – Cameron Grey
Your Wicked Ways – Becky Shaheen
Dancing With The Devil – EMO
I Feel Like I'm Drowning – Two Feet
Ghost Town – Benson Boone
La Canción – Maye
Two Waves – The Prams
La Corriente – Bad Bunny, Tony Dize
Angels Like You – Miley Cyrus
Lost My Mind – FiloChill
The Night We Met – Lord Huron
I'll Be Good – Jaymes Young
Lost Without You – Freya Ridings
Who Do You Want – Ex Habit
I Want To – Rosenfeld

Baby You're Worth It – Kina
I Wanna Go Down With You – Russ
I'll Make You Love Me – Kat Leon
Bad Girl – Daya
Love Is A Bitch – Two Feet
Pushin – Vella
Power – Isak Danielson

SEEDS OF SORROW RECAP

Don's words were ringing in her ears. The room was beginning to look fuzzy, like she was looking through a cloudy lens. Hadina reached for her hand but Peyton pulled away, needing space. She tried not to let the hurt on Hadina's face bother her, even though she knew it would make her upset later.

"I don't understand," Peyton heard herself saying, but her voice didn't sound like her own. The world around her felt strange and deceptive and she wanted to throw up.

"It's a long story, *cariña*," Don said, placing his hand on her shoulder. She shook him off and stood, pacing across the plush carpet.

"*Papi...*"

"Tell me the fucking truth, Don!"

"I knew Demi a long, long time ago. When it was decided that you'd be put up for adoption, I helped make it happen. You were just an innocent kid and I wanted to make sure you were safe."

Peyton stopped pacing and caught his gaze. While he seemed genuine, her gut was telling her that he was trying to placate her with half truths. She shook her head. "Tell me the full story."

Don sighed. It looked like he wanted to plead with her, but the fiery glare she was giving him was enough to stop him in his tracks. She leaned against the wall with her arms folded—as far away from both Don and Hadina as she could get without leaving the room—and motioned for him to start talking.

"Demi used to date one of my employees. Isaac was one of the most loyal, intelligent people I've ever known, but he let his guard down. During one of our infiltration ops, he came across Demi and the *pendejo* fell in love."

A lump caught in the back of Peyton's throat. "Isaac is my father?"

Don nodded, not meeting her gaze. "They met up in secret for months. He loved her so much, but I don't think Demi has ever loved anyone in her life. Isaac was foolish and didn't see that Demi was just using him, getting bits of information out of him that could help her climb the ranks of the drug world."

"What happened to him?"

"There was a meet that went wrong and Isaac was caught in the crossfire. He bled out before we could save him." Don looked up at Peyton, tears glazing over his eyes. "*Lo siento.* I still carry the pain of his death with me every day."

Peyton felt herself going weak at the knees. She gripped the wall behind her and closed her eyes, pushing her tears down. There was more she needed to hear before she could let herself feel anything.

"Demi found out she was pregnant after Isaac died. She didn't want to be a mother, and I couldn't bear to see my friend's baby come to any harm. So, I convinced her to put you up for adoption."

Peyton scoffed, shaking her head in disbelief. "Demi Treyva doesn't seem like the kind of person to listen to advice."

"She doesn't. But she loves money and power."

"You *bought* me?" Peyton yelled, pushing off the wall. "What the actual fuck?"

Don held up his hands in silent surrender, sensing the rage simmering beneath her skin. "I didn't buy you. I bribed Demi into putting you up for adoption. It was the only way to ensure she didn't ruin your life."

"This is the most fucked-up thing I've ever heard. And what? You've just been keeping tabs on me all these years?" A thought dawned on her then, nausea flooding her system. She looked at Don, horrified. "You knew. That day we met at the hospital... You *knew* me."

He at least had the decency to look ashamed. He glanced at Hadina but her face was stone, her eyes blank as she looked at him. Peyton couldn't bear to look at Hadina for more than a moment, for fear that she'd run over and collapse into the other woman's arms.

"*Sí, lo sabia.* I knew who you were."

Bile rose up the back of Peyton's throat and she doubled over, clutching her stomach. "Oh my God! I can't—you could have told me. But instead, you kept it a secret for all these months. You let me fall in love with your daughter! Fuck, you let me go to that meeting, knowing Demi was my mother!"

Hadina had moved from the sofa to Peyton's side. She began to rub circles on the bottom of her back, and for a moment, Peyton leaned into the touch, desperate for comfort from someone safe and familiar.

But maybe Hadina wasn't safe either.

Peyton lurched back, moving towards the door. Every step Hadina took towards her, Peyton took two in the opposite direction. She put a hand out in front of her, urging her to stop. "Don't come near me!"

Hadina flinched and stepped back as though she'd been slapped. "Peyton, it's me. I would never hurt you. I had no idea about any of this!"

The pain in Hadina's voice was her breaking point, and Peyton finally allowed the tears to fall. Her entire body ached as though it had been waiting for the release. She looked at Hadina through an onslaught of tears, her shoulders shaking as she sobbed.

"I don't know that, though, do I? How can I ever trust a member of this family after everything I've just learned?"

"*Tentadora*, please," Hadina pleaded, her voice cracking on the words. "You can trust me. I promise you that."

Peyton shook her head. "I'll never be able to trust anyone again," she sobbed, wiping her eyes with her sleeves. "I can't be here right now. I need some space."

Spinning on her heels, Peyton ran through the house and out onto the street. She gasped, inhaling as much fresh air into her lungs as possible. She continued to run until she was sure Hadina wasn't following her before collapsing onto a bench. Her chest heaved as she tried to catch her breath, to calm herself long enough to stop her tears from falling.

She didn't know how this was her life. It was crazy to the point of insanity and she was tempted to say that it was all in her head, some elaborate nightmare that she couldn't wake up from. But the look of despair in Don's eyes, the heartbreak in Hadina's... It was too real to be fake.

All her life, she'd grown up in a dysfunctional family unit. The only saving grace was her beautiful Melina. And despite the feeling of being an interloper in her own family, she'd never craved the knowledge of who her birth parents were. When she was old enough to ask about them, she did so only because she knew it was expected. And when she was told that the records were sealed, she was secretly relieved. She didn't want to know about the people who'd given her up, had discarded her like she was nothing.

But somehow the truth that she had so desperately avoided had been flung in her face and it was so, so much worse than she had ever anticipated.

If it weren't bad enough that her birth mother was a psychotic, evil, cold-hearted bitch who was willing to do anything to be on top, her birth father had been a good man and was dead. He'd fallen in love with the wrong person and karma punished him instead of *her*.

And Don knew about it all. For months, he'd comforted Peyton and made her feel like she was a part of his family. Meanwhile, he knew that she belonged to another.

Falling onto the grass in front of the bench, Peyton sat on her knees and retched. Her throat burned by the time she'd emptied the contents of her stomach, her eyes stinging from the tears that wouldn't stop falling. Peyton had no idea what she was going to do. She barely spoke to her parents, and even the mere thought of returning home to Willowbrooks made it feel like she had phantom hands around her throat, choking the life out of her. The Adis family had become hers, and without them, she didn't have anyone.

Her phone rang in her pocket, vibrating against her leg. She sniffled and wiped at her eyes before pulling it out, half-expecting to see Hadina blowing up her voicemail. Instead, the incoming call was from Kaira. Peyton clicked the screen and accepted the call. "Kaira?"

"Peyton! Are you okay? Piper called me and told me what happened. I don't even have words."

"I'm o—" Peyton choked on the words and burst into a fresh flood of tears.

"Oh, honey," Kaira cooed. "It's going to be okay. Where are you? I can get Piper to pick you up and bring you to my place."

Panic seized Peyton's throat. "No! I don't want to be near a single person in that family right now. I don't know what to do, Kaira."

"Okay, here's what you're going to do. I'm gonna text you my address and you'll call an Uber or something to get you here. I promise not to tell Piper where you are. But I need to know you're safe, so you can hide out at my apartment until you sort your head out."

"Thank you," Peyton sobbed into the phone.

Kaira tutted. "It's nothing, honey. That's what friends are for. I'll see you soon."

Once the call ended, Peyton picked herself up from the ground. Her face was puffy and sore, so she could only imagine how she looked. The phone chimed with a text message from Kaira, a drop pin to her apartment. Peyton clicked on the location and saw that it was only a few blocks from where she was presently. She took in a deep breath, the fresh air filling her lungs and helping to soothe her addled brain.

She'd walk to Kaira's. She needed the time to think.

Pulling maps up on her phone, Peyton took off in the direction of Kaira's place. The night air was cold against her raw cheeks, burning into her chest as she breathed. There hadn't been time to grab a jacket or comfortable shoes or any of her stuff before fleeing, and she was now beginning to see how woefully unprepared she was.

Unprepared for a life on the run.

Peyton didn't know if that really was the case or not, but it's how it felt in her heart. She knew that Hadina wouldn't let her go without a fight; she'd told her as much when they'd first met. It seemed like a lifetime ago since she had walked into that office and saw Hadina strapping up, looking like she was preparing for war. If only Peyton had listened to her head instead of her heart and fled the moment Hadina had left that night, she wouldn't be in this fucked-up mess now.

Peyton heaved a sigh and checked her phone. She was only five minutes away from Kaira's apartment, somewhere she could sit and be alone with her thoughts.

Turning the corner onto the next street, she was surprised to see that all the streetlamps were flickering on and off. Unease settled into her gut as she continued on, using the flashlight on her phone to see where she was going. It was a dark evening with no stars or moon to be seen in the sky, making it difficult to see more than a few feet ahead of her.

She swore under her breath when the streetlight above her sparked, the bulb cutting out completely. Chills worked their way down her spine, a thousand needlepoints scratching at her skin. She shivered and wrapped her free arm around her stomach, picking up the pace as she walked.

She'd almost reached the corner to the next street when tires screeched from behind her, making her jump out of her skin. Turning around, she caught sight of a black van speeding down the road. She pressed up against the closest gate, looking for somewhere she could hide. Dread settled in her stomach and adrenaline kicked in, propelling her forward.

Sprinting as fast as she could under the poor lighting and with even poorer footwear, Peyton tried to outrun the vehicle. She knew it was stupid, that she wasn't fast enough, but it didn't stop her from trying. Just like how she knew said vehicle was coming after her.

As she was about to turn the corner, she tripped up over the uneven sidewalk, falling flat on her face. She tried to push herself up but pain shot up her leg, radiating around her ankle. She must have twisted it as she fell. There was nothing she could do as the van skidded to a halt on the sidewalk, the side door flying open.

Two large figures jumped out, their faces covered with black masks. They grabbed Peyton by the arms and hauled her to her feet, shoving her forward with unnecessary force. She fought against them, but their grip on her was iron-tight, and she could feel her skin beginning to bruise already.

"Let me go!" Peyton bellowed at the top of her lungs, kicking her legs out beneath her.

Her struggling made no difference as they threw her into the van and climbed in beside her. There was another hidden figure inside, who leaned forward before shoving a hood over Peyton's head. The material was rough and scratchy against her skin and smelled like sweat and sawdust.

She continued to scream as the door closed and she felt the vehicle move again. Hands grabbed her by the shoulders and wrists, rope being tied tight to bind her. She kicked out with her uninjured foot, only to have it shoved back.

"You made this too easy, you know," a voice said. It was a man's voice, rough and crackly like he was a chain-smoker.

"Yeah, didn't your mommy ever teach you not to walk alone in the dark?" another voice chimed in, earning a chuckle from Old Smokey.

Peyton screamed and kicked out again, her foot connecting with what felt like a stomach. The man let out an annoyed *oof* and grabbed the hood, seizing a bunch of her hair in the process.

"You little bastard!"

"Go fuck yourself," Peyton seethed, wriggling her wrists to see if she could get free of the rope.

"You'll pay for that," Old Smokey rasped in her ear, before slamming her head into the door. When it was obvious she hadn't passed out, he did it again.

Pain radiated through Peyton's head, her ears ringing. Black spots swam in her eyes and her vision blurred. Slowly and painfully, unconsciousness pulled her under until there was nothing but darkness surrounding her. When her eyes fluttered shut, the last thing she saw was Hadina's face. Peyton was slipping into the shadows but Hadina was *la reina de las sombras* and she'd keep her little temptress safe there.

TRANSLATIONS

Tentadora = Temptress

Mi querida, por favor = My dear, please

¡No, basta! = No, stop it!

Cálmate = Calm down

No más llanto = No more crying

¿Dónde estás? = Where are you?

Entonces pongámonos a trabajar = Let's get to work

¡Escúchame con mucha atención! = Listen to me very carefully!

¡Ella es familia! = She is family!

¡Ella es mi corazón y la amo! = She is my heart and I love her!

¡Cierra la puta boca! = Shut the fuck up!

¡Detener! = Stop!

Jefa = Boss

Tengo esto = I have this

Lo siento, cariña = I'm sorry, dear

Regresa a mí = Come back to me

Reina de las sombras = Queen of the shadows

El diablo = The devil

Mierda = Shit

¡No olvides quién es la jefa! = Don't forget who is boss!

¿Que demonios estas haciendo aquí? = What the hell are you doing here?

Hola, hermana = Hello, sister

Eres un desastre = You're a disaster

¿Qué deseas? = What do you want?

Puta = Bitch

El amor te ha hecho débil = Love has made you weak

Este dolor hace que me duela el corazón de la misma manera que lo hizo perder a Mami = This pain makes my heart hurt the same way losing Mom did

Entiendo = I understand

Yo te ayudo = I will help you

Entonces habla = Then speak

Protegemos a los inocentes = We protect the innocent

¿Entonces qué pasó? = So, what happened?

Perra psicótica = Psychotic bitch

Bastarda = Bastard

La tentadora de las sombras = The temptress of the shadows

Pinche panocha = Fucking pussy

Mi amor = My love

Te seguiría al inframundo = I would follow you to the underworld

¿Qué ocurre? = What's happening?

Eres una tonta = You're a fool

¡Dios mío! = My God!

Conozco tu alma = I know your soul

Buenos días = Good morning

¡Necia! = Stubborn / Infuriating

Siempre = Always

¡Pégame! = Hit me!

Niñita = Little girl

¡Haz algo al respecto! = Do something about it!

¿Tu me entiendes? = You understand me?

Me la voy a chingotiar = I'm going to fuck her up

Como quieras = Whatever you want

Ella está a salvo = She's safe

Me aseguré de ello = I made sure of it

Hablar pronto = Talk soon

Ta bueno = It's good

Hermano = Brother

Tienes razón = You're right

¿Entender? = Understand?

Hijo! = An expression used for dang it / yikes

Yo ah pasado por ríos de sangre! = I have been through rivers of blood!

He hecho tantas cosas que no podrías comprender = I've done so many things you wouldn't understand

¡No eres una niña estúpida, así que deja de actuar como tal! = You're not a stupid little girl, so stop acting like one!

¡Déjame explicarte antes de juzgar la situación! = Let me explain before you judge the situation!

Terca! = Stubborn

Dios ayúdame = God help me

Pendejo = Idiot

Mi belleza = My beauty

¡Bien! = Good!

Mejor verte = Better to see you

¿Quién es ella? = Who is she?

Señor ten piedad = Lord have mercy

Güera = White girl

Te he extrañado, mija = I have missed you, my girl

Te he extrañado más, papi = I've missed you more, daddy

No te respondo = I don't answer to you

Recuerda con quién estás hablando, hermano = Remember who you're talking to, brother

¿Qué? ¿Cuyo nombre? = What? Whose name?

No finjas que no te estás tirando a esa linda chica blanca = Don't pretend you're not fucking that pretty, white girl

Cachondo = Horny

Sí, soy de ella = Yes, I'm hers

Chinga tu madre! = Fuck you!

Sí, ella tiene razón = Yes, she's right

Mucho gusto = Nice to meet you

Esta es mi novia = This is my girlfriend

¿Qué pasa, hija? = What's wrong, daughter?

Claro, mijita = Of course, my daughter

No manches = No way!

Blancita = White girl

Pinche perra = Fucking bitch

¡Patética! = Pathetic

¡Manten tu boca cerrada! = Keep your mouth shut!

Te prometo que = I promise you

Juntos = Together

Pinche puta madre = Fucking motherfucker

Mi reina, tenga paciencia! = My queen, be patient!

Eres una vasca = You're a scumbag

Cabrón = Bastard

Hermanita = Little sister

Sé a la luz = Be in the light

Estaté queta = Be still

¡Consigue una habitación! = Get a room!

La tenemos = We have her

¿Qué has hecho? = What have you done?

POEM

The shadow world had welcomed her,
And made her feel like she was home.
The light inside her lived,
But the darkness meant she was no longer alone.
She had grown comfortable in the dark,
And fallen in love with the queen.
Never before had the goddess
Felt herself be so seen.
But fate is as cruel as winter nights
And foresight they did not possess.
Death and lies were quick to spread,
Leading to the capture of the beloved goddess.
The family would unite as one,
A quest to save the goddess that could not fail.
But as with all heroic stories,
Theirs is covered in branches of betrayal.

CHAPTER 1

HADINA

TIME WAS MOVING TOO SLOWLY FOR HADINA AS SHE PACED THE HALLWAY outside of her office. People always compared time to molasses, but it reminded her of the thick, stickiness of blood as congealed below a dead body.

"Fuck!" she screamed, slamming her hand against the wall. Thinking of dead bodies just made her mind conjure cruel images of her *tentadora*'s dead, bloodied body and it made her want to set fire to the world while she bathed in the ashes.

Four hours.

Four painstakingly slow hours was how long it had been since Peyton ran away from Hadina and her fucked up family. *Give her the time she asked for,* her father had advised, but Hadina wasn't a patient woman and she didn't like being told what to do.

Since the moment Peyton had stepped foot inside the family home, she had cast a spell over Hadina and captured her every thought. Without her, it felt like someone was pressing on her throat and Hadina had never much liked being on the receiving end of being choked.

She felt the presence of her father behind her back before he made any noise to alert her. "Hadina."

Her heart ached at the pain in his voice, but anger burned in her veins and she longed to let it erupt, destroying everything in her wake.

"Please don't, *Papi*. I can't speak to you right now. I can't even look at you."

"*Mi querida, por favor*. It was a complicated situation and I did what I thought was best."

Hadina spun on her heels and leveled her gaze at the person she had once trusted more than anyone in the world. She could see how apologetic he was, but saying sorry didn't make everything better. There weren't enough bandaids in the world to cover the wound he had opened back up, knowing it would mean she'd have to watch the woman she loved bleed.

"*¡No, basta!* I can't hear this right now, *Papi*. If you keep talking, keep making excuses, I won't be able to keep myself from hating you for being the reason she left. And I don't want to hate you, but if I've lost her forever because of secrets *you* chose to keep... I just can't, okay?"

Her voice cracked as she swallowed down her tears. She wouldn't cry, not yet. Everything was not lost. She would get Peyton back and they would destroy Demi Treyva—*together*.

"There's still things you need to—" Her father got cut off as the front door slammed open, a wild-eyed Kaira standing in the doorway.

"Hadina!"

"Kaira? What's wrong?'"

Kaira stormed forward, tears rolling down her cheeks. "Something's happened to her."

A cold chill ran down Hadina's spine. "Tell me everything."

Kaira slumped down onto the bottom stair of the grand staircase, wiping her cheeks with the back of her hands as she relayed her phone call with Peyton. That had been *hours* ago and Kaira... Hadina knew she couldn't lash out at her best friend, but the urge to hurt her for waiting so long to contact them was overwhelming. If it wasn't for the fact that she was a sniffling mess, Hadina thought she honestly might have grabbed Kaira by the hair and repeatedly slammed her into the banister.

But she had more important things to worry about.

"I figured she just needed some more time! Or that maybe she had come home. But then an hour passed...and another, and another. Fuck, Hadina, I'm so sorry! I don't know what to do or where she could be."

"You said she told you where she was when she called you, right? We'll go there first. While we look, I'll have the team pull up CCTV of that area and we'll find out where she is. They should be able to track her phone."

Kaira gulped, blowing her nose into a tissue. Mascara was running down her cheeks, leaving dark marks against her skin. Hadina had seen her in tears many times over the course of their friendship, but she'd never seen her look honestly terrified. Not even when Hadina had threatened her—which hurt her ego a little, but that was besides the point.

"Kai, stop, *cálmate. No más llanto.* It's not your fault. We'll find her."

Nodding, Kaira wiped her tears again and stood, blowing out a slow breath to compose herself. "Let's go."

"Give me a minute, okay? Go fill in Piper and Harris while I get some stuff from the office."

She walked into the office and closed the door behind her, letting out a staggering breath as she collapsed backwards. She wanted to scream or cry or throw something, but instead she just sat there. Staring. Unmoving. Unfeeling. If she let herself do anything other than sit in the silence of the room, Hadina knew she would break. And the last thing she had time for was analyzing her own emotions.

"Why did you have to leave me? I could have kept you safe!" Hadina whispered to herself, wishing Peyton could hear her.

It had taken a lot of arguing to get Harris to stay behind with Piper. While having her Second with her was always the preferable option, the man had a gunshot wound to his shoulder and Hadina knew rest was essential for the healing process. Besides, he would be able to command their team from her office and if anyone knew what the next steps were without her having to tell them, it was Harris.

"Is Adrian okay?"

Hadina glanced at Kaira from the corner of her eye as she drove, nodding her head slightly. "He's had worse bullet wounds than that. But it's still an inconvenience to him, me, and the company. Pip sewed him up though, so I'm sure he'll be fighting fit soon."

A silence settled between them as Hadina turned onto the street where Peyton had last been, according to what she had told Kaira. She parked the car and jumped out, immediately scanning the area for some sort of sign. The delusional part of her brain was telling Hadina that maybe Peyton had fallen asleep on a bench somewhere. Shock did insane things to the body and exhaustion was certainly plausible.

Plausible, but still not reality.

"*¿Dónde estás, tentadora?*" Hadina whispered quietly, closing her eyes against the fluorescent light of the streetlamp.

"Hadina! Come over here!" Kaira shouted to her from the

corner of the street. As Hadina got closer, Kaira pointed forward. "There's skid marks across the road down there, look!"

Hadina broke into a run—something she had perfected in stilettos, though she knew her feet wouldn't thank her for it when she hit old age—and let out a string of curses in barely comprehensible Spanish. Tire marks had churned out parts of the grassy sidewalk, which meant the vehicle had gone off-road. There were only a few reasons for that and combined with the burnt rubber on the road, Hadina's stomach sank with realization.

"Someone came after her. This was a bag and grab. FUCK!"

Pulling her phone from her pocket, Hadina dialed Harris who answered before the first ring. "Boss—"

"She's been snatched."

"Yes. Street cameras were taken out beforehand, but we managed to catch sight of a 2017 Chevrolet Express van speeding a couple streets away. They were driving erratic as fuck and it looked like the driver had some sort of mask on. It had to be them."

"Did you get a clear look at the plates?"

"Yes, boss. I have someone doing a scan right now and we'll see if we can trace it. We tried to tap Peyton's phone too, but the fuckers must've turned it off. The last ping is from the cell tower closest to where y'all are."

Hadina took a steadying breath and spoke into the phone, "I need you to find her, Adrian. I don't know what I'd—"

"Hey, we'll find her. Everyone on the team loves her, and so does your family. Peyton is one of us and we won't let her get away." Harris cleared his throat, the sound crackling down the receiver. "Now, with all due respect, get your shit together. We've got work to do, boss."

"*Entonces pongámonos a trabajar.*"

CHAPTER 2

PEYTON

"How hard did you hit her? She's been out for ages!"

"Nah, she woke up earlier and screamed like a banshee. I shoved the rag in her mouth to get her to shut the fuck up. She must've passed out again at some point, but I'm not taking the heat for smacking her around."

One of the voices chuckled hoarsely. "Regina did say to get her by whatever means necessary. I figure roughing her up a bit is just part of the process. If she wanted her in one piece and unharmed, Regina would've sent a fucking limo for her."

Peyton kept her eyes closed and her breathing steady as she listened to the bastards who had kidnapped her.

Her head was throbbing and her throat was so dry that it felt as though she'd swallowed a gallon of sand.

She had no idea how long it had been since she was chased down by the van and a bag was stuffed over her head, but Peyton felt like it had been an age. Some time ago, her tears had dried up and she had stopped begging to be let go. Whoever her captors were, they weren't going to change their minds. They were on Demi's payroll, and they didn't seem the types to want to swap vocations.

It felt like a slap as she thought about that woman and the layers of deception she'd concealed her life with.

Demi Treyva. Her *biological mother*.

What a cruel fucking joke.

Peyton had been passed around foster families throughout her early years, each one subjecting her to a different kind of torture. When she was finally adopted by her parents, she thought that it meant the start of a better, brighter future. But it didn't work out like that.

Kids who come from the system aren't damaged goods, but the world treats them like that. Peyton's parents wanted to fix her, wanted to make her a perfect little lady who never misbehaved. But with the trauma she had endured before being adopted, Peyton couldn't act like the angel child her parents wanted her to be.

No, instead she lashed out. She hated being touched—especially by her adoptive father, who used an aftershave that was a bit too close to the one she'd be smelling for hours after her foster brother left her room in the middle of the night, her silent cries tasting like the salty tears which stained her cheeks.

Now that she was an adult and had figured out her own ways of coping, she felt pangs of guilt whenever she thought of her father. He had been the one to raise her for the better part of her life, and he had never once blamed her for how she reacted to him whenever he tried to hug her or put his hand on her shoulder. But she blamed herself. Every time he'd hug her big sister, she'd feel the jealousy burning up inside of her, but it didn't change how her body reacted every single time.

And her mom...Peyton wished she didn't resent her the way

she did. But her mom had adopted a kid from the system, and it was the entirely wrong thing to do. She didn't know how to handle a child with *any* sort of issue, never-mind the long list Peyton brought with her. When she lashed out, her mom would yell which only made Peyton angry *and* upset. But the times she didn't yell were worse. Silence was a punishment and Peyton found that she hated being alone with her own thoughts. It was like her mom sensed that and doubled down, learning over time that the only way to really hurt Peyton and get her to behave was to let her stew in the dark palace of her mind.

Her parents weren't bad people. They were severely inexperienced and privileged. Their lives had been easy and the biological child they had was perfect. They wanted a clone of her, and Peyton resembled her adoptive sister an eerie amount. They say you have a doppelgänger somewhere in the world, and it was like fate had messed up the timeline somehow, stalling her birth a few years too late. When she first met Melina, it was like looking in a mirror, though the features of the older girl showed more maturity.

Still, Peyton loved her adoptive parents. They had taken her in, given her a home and a safe place. If she was a normal girl with a normal childhood, she'd have thrived in the environment they gave her. But Peyton was complicated and the only person who could deal with her was Melina. Her darling big sister, her best friend, the hand helping to guide her through the darkness.

But Melina was dead. She'd *chosen* to leave Peyton, and that hurt more than anything she'd been through in her short twenty-one years.

Melina was her hand in the dark, but somehow she hadn't noticed her darkness seeping into the light her sister created. Peyton would never be able to forgive herself for not noticing just how badly her sister was hurting. She always seemed happy, striving to make the world a better place.

Until she wasn't happy anymore.

She wasn't anything.

A floating corpse in a river of blood, and Peyton had been the one to hold her as she found her lifeless body, the sea of red seeping into her soul.

Melina was the only thing that made her home feel like *home*. Losing her meant losing part of herself, and watching her parents grieve for the child they cherished. Peyton couldn't be a replica of Melina in life, and she definitely couldn't be her replacement in death.

So, Peyton had left and started her life over. A fresh start. Someplace new, with no ties to Willowbrooks.

Or so she thought. Because somehow her life had imploded and now she knew more about her biological parents than she ever wanted to. If she could erase the knowledge from her mind, she would.

But no. Her life was a cosmic fuck-up and Demi Treyva was her biological mother. A backwards karmic joke, that's what it was.

Though, Peyton wasn't laughing.

No, she was tied to a chair with a dirty rag in her mouth as a gag, her body bruised and aching. A prisoner, in captivity at the hands of the person who gave her life. What a fucking *joke*.

The chime of a text message broke through her thoughts. Peyton slowly opened her eyes, keeping her head forward and tilted at an angle so that the men wouldn't know she was awake just yet. One of the men nudged the other with his elbow, showing him the phone.

"Regina is outside." *Old Smokey*, Peyton thought to herself, remembering the rough voice.

His partner in crime grinned, showing off his crooked teeth. "Time for some fun, then."

Peyton listened to their heavy footsteps retreat before she let herself breathe, stretching her neck as she looked around her. They were in some sort of abandoned house. Dust clung to the walls and coated every surface. The old fireplace had been boarded up but the wood was old and rotten, breaking away in parts that lay discarded on the floor. The wallpaper had marks on it from frames that were long gone and there was no sign of any furniture around. Peyton figured it had been a long time since anyone had lived in the house and somehow, she didn't think there was a caretaker looking after the place.

"I see you're awake."

She had been so lost in her thoughts that she hadn't heard Demi arrive in the room. Not dignifying her with a response, Peyton kept her mouth shut as she waited for Demi to come into view. Her gag was roughly pulled from her mouth, causing Peyton to choke on the sudden freedom to breathe properly.

"What? No '*thank you*'? No '*I love you*' for your momma?"

Peyton narrowed her eyes. "Have you known all this time?"

Demi laughed, dragging a chair into the room with her. Her blonde hair was tucked behind her ears, showing off the sharp features of her pretty face. It was a pity she was so beautiful on the outside and so rotten on the inside.

"God, no. I thought I had sorted out that little problem long ago. It was a shock to see you at the restaurant with the Adis crew."

"What the hell does that mean? Sorted that problem long ago? You literally gave me up for adoption."

"And yet," Demi said, waving her hand in Peyton's direction, "here you are. Fucking up my entire organisation with the help of that entitled little bitch of yours."

A growl hissed through Peyton's teeth at the disrespect of Hadina. "Don't talk about her like that!"

Demi grinned, showing off her perfectly straight, perfectly white teeth. She looked like a predator, waiting to pounce. "Aw, you really are in love aren't you? How foolish. Let's just hope that love of yours is reciprocated, because I'm counting on the type of wrath that only a lover can have."

Peyton tried to lunge forward, fighting against her bindings. "You won't touch her!"

"Oh, darling, I don't need to lay a hand on Hadina to cause the type of pain I have in mind. She thinks she's a queen, but she's just playing dress up. No, I'm going to show her the pain of losing the person she loves most." Standing from her chair, Demi walked over to Peyton, running her finger softly across the cheek of her daughter. "I'm going to break Hadina Adis until she's an empty shell. And then I'm going to crush her and watch as she shatters beneath my heel."

Pulling back, Demi crouched in front of Peyton, meeting her eye level. "But first... I think I should introduce myself properly. Let me show you the love of a mother's touch, darling daughter."

Peyton opened her mouth to inform her that she was her mother by genetics only, but she didn't get the chance to say anything. Demi was quick as she backhanded her, the rings on her fingers cutting into Peyton's skin as they connected with her cheek. The force behind the slap threw Peyton's head back, apparently creating the perfect angle for Demi's fist to connect with her chin.

She groaned as the chair fell backwards, her head thumping off the wooden floor. Her breath came out in a painful whimper as blood trickled from her mouth.

"Pick her up," Demi demanded to someone. Suddenly, Peyton was being lifted—still attached to the chair by the ropes biting into her skin—by Old Smokey. The disgusting odor he emitted filled Peyton's nostrils and made her gag.

Grabbing her by the hair, Demi pulled her head back so that she was sneering mere inches from her face. "Tell me, Peyton, am I everything you hoped I would be?"

A cruel smile spread across the woman's face as she brought

her arm back, swinging her fist into Peyton's face again. She felt all the anger and hatred from her childhood rise to the surface again as the hits continued. A thousand vows of revenge filled her mind until unconsciousness finally blanketed her.

CHAPTER 3

Hadina

Hadina was filled with a level of rage she didn't know she possessed as she listened to one of her men make excuses down the phone. She slammed her hand down on her desk, ignoring the needles of pain that shot through her bones.

"I don't fucking care! *¡Escúchame con mucha atención!* I do not give a flying fuck how difficult it is. They didn't just disappear. Find them or I swear I will skin you al-"

"Hadina!"

Piper's admonishment cut Hadina off in the middle of her threat. If it had been anyone else other than her little sister, she'd have contemplated using her dagger to make a point. But as it was, Piper was one of only two people who could get Hadina to do what they wanted.

But the other person was the love of her life who was probably being tortured just for being part of her life. So, Piper was treading dangerous ground because Hadina had never felt so unstable in her entire life.

"Just do what she's asking. Next time I won't stop her from saying *or* carrying out her threats," Piper said before hitting to end the call. She turned to Hadina with a disappointed look on her face. "You have got to calm down, Hadina. Screaming at the people helping you isn't going to do anything."

Hadina glared at her sister, trying to force herself to cool down. She drummed her fingertips against the edge of her desk, but her thoughts were consumed with Peyton. Every time she allowed herself more than a second to breathe, her mind conjured images of the terrible things Peyton was enduring. While she couldn't know for sure, she knew what *she* would be doing to a prisoner...

"Don't tell me what to do, Piper. Please, just leave me alone."

Piper sat in the chair across from the desk, crossing her arms as she looked at her sister. "Oh, don't start that shit with me. And you being on your own right now is quite literally a terrible idea. Did you even hear the way you were speaking to one of the people on your own team?"

Pinching the bridge of her nose, Hadina took a steadying breath. She loved Piper, but if she didn't stop trying to organize her like she was some sort of lost puppy, she was going to snap.

"I did, yes. Because I have been running my team for years, Piper. Remember how you didn't want to be part of Adis & Co.? Well, it means you don't have to get involved when I'm talking to *my* team."

"Screw you, Hadina. I'm involved because it's not just some random *puta* that's been taken. Peyton is one of us. *¡Ella es familia!* This has nothing to do with the company."

"Of course she's not just some girl. *¡Ella es mi corazón y la amo!* I'm not fucking around, Piper. I'll handle this however I see fit!"

"What's with all the shouting?"

Hadina rolled her eyes as Harris walked into the office, his wounded shoulder held up across his chest with a sling. He looked at Piper with a soft expression before turning to Hadina with a steely gaze. "Why are you yelling? What do you need me to do, boss?"

"She's threatening your team and being fucking unhinged because she's barely sleeping."

"*¡Cierra la puta boca!*"

"*¡Detener!* Enough, Hadina! Don't speak to her like that."

"Adrian, I don't know who the fuck you think you-"

Piper jumped from her chair and stormed from the room, slamming the office door behind her. Hadina sighed, resting her head in her hands. She heard Harris take a seat in the chair Piper had just vacated, letting out a small groan as he moved his arm and disturbed the wound.

"Hadina, seriously, what the fuck? I've never heard you speak to Piper like that and I've known you my entire life."

"I know," Hadina said softly, rubbing her temples. Guilt churned in her stomach at her actions, but it somehow did not outweigh the absolute devastation she was feeling at the loss of Peyton in her life. She knew in her heart that she would get her back, but also knew that Peyton wouldn't be the same when they did. "I'll apologize to her."

Harris sighed. "Hadina, you can't do all of this on your own. You're going to run yourself into the ground. We need you to be on top of your game if we wanna get Peyton back."

"Adrian, I... I don't know how to do this. I've never cared about anyone the way I have about her. You know what we've done to people. Can you imagine that being done to her?" Hadina's voice broke and she cursed herself internally for being so weak. "Demi is going to break her and I don't think I'm a good enough person to be able to piece her back together."

Harris leaned forward in his chair and using his uninjured arm, he took hold of Hadina's hand. She was tempted to throw him off, but she honestly didn't have the energy to keep fighting.

"You're the strongest person I know, Hadina. But you know what? Peyton is strong as hell too. She can absolutely handle whatever Demi throws at her. Hell, she fell in love with you so the girl obviously loves to live life on the edge."

She couldn't help the snort that escaped at his attempt at a joke, but it turned into a strangled sob at the back of her throat. "I can't lose her."

"We won't let that happen. But you've got to sort your shit out, *jefa*."

Hadina nodded and stood, wiping her face with the backs of her hands. Throwing her hair over her shoulders, she steeled herself and forced herself to become the Hadina Adis everyone knew her to be.

"*Tengo esto.* But first, I'm going to apologize to my baby sister."

<hr>

MAKING HER WAY UPSTAIRS, HADINA TOOK HER TIME TO CONSIDER WHAT she was going to say to her sister in apology. She hated that she'd snapped at her, and hated the fact that she had sounded a bit too much like Zelina.

Stopping outside Piper's bedroom door, she tapped lightly. She knew Piper was inside from the light filtering under the doorway, but her sister didn't answer.

"Pip, I know you're in there."

"Go away, Hadina."

Hadina rolled her eyes, suddenly transported back to when they were teenagers. It wasn't the first time she'd stood outside this door, waiting for entry so she could beg forgiveness for her quick temper.

"Piper, I'm coming in."

She opened the door and the sight before her caved her chest wide open. Sitting on top of her duvet, Piper was curled up by her headboard, sobbing into one of the turquoise throw pillows. Mascara streaked down her pale cheeks, black smudges staining her chest and the pillow she clutched there.

"What happened to that tough girl who just yelled at me? I think I liked her."

Piper sniffled, wiping her nose with a tissue from her nightstand. "You yelled back at her! If you liked that version of me so much, maybe you should go work shit out with Zellie."

"Oh, Pip," Hadina said, making her way inside the room. She closed the door behind her and walked over to the plush bed, kicking off her heels before climbing up beside her little sister. "*Lo siento, cariña.* I was an asshole and I'm sorry for taking my pain out on you."

"I'm worried too, you know. I know Peyton is, like, your person...but she's my friend too, Hadina. Besides Kaira, she's one of the only people who know about our life and didn't run for the hills. She's family and I'm worried too."

The dam of her tears burst again and Piper buried her face in her hands. Hadina pulled her by the shoulder and enveloped her in a hug, rubbing circles across her back.

"I know, Pip. I know. I was being selfish. I just—this is new to me. *Caring* is new to me. I feel like my chest is being ripped open and there's nothing I can do but bleed out."

Hadina hadn't expected to make such an admission and the honesty of it took her aback. It seemed like Peyton had created a new, softer side of her and she couldn't bury it, no matter how hard she tried.

Pulling back a little so she could look at her, Piper caught Hadina's gaze. The pity in her eyes was abundant but honestly, Hadina was pitying herself too. She thought she was going to be able to keep it together but the second Piper leaned forward for another hug, Hadina found herself crying too.

"I hate this, you know. I hate being weak and emotional."

"Hadina, emotions don't make you weak. Your love is what will save her."

"I'm scared, Piper," Hadina admitted solemnly. "The last time I was this scared, *Mami* was sick and we lost her. I can't love someone so deeply and go through that loss again."

Piper sighed and grabbed a few tissues for each of them. Hadina dabbed at her eyes and let out a soft chuckle as Piper blew her nose loudly, competing with an elephant for noise level.

"Losing *Mami* was something none of us will ever get over. But it doesn't mean you should shut yourself away from emotions so you don't get hurt. You realize that you admitted to me earlier that you loved her?" Hadina's eyes widened and Piper shook her head. "Yeah, I didn't think you'd have realized what you said. But you did. You were so busy yelling that you just let it slip."

Hadina blew out a breath and leaned her head back against the wooden frame. She let her admission settle for a second, contemplating her feelings for once.

"I was so angry and frustrated and worried... I just let it all out at once. But yes, I love her. I'm not ashamed of that, even if it does make me terrified."

Piper smiled, taking Hadina's hand in hers and squeezing softly. "Stop letting fear rule your life. If you love her, you'll do anything to get her back. And Hadi, nobody loves as fiercely as you. It doesn't matter what version of Peyton we get back—you'll be the one to help her heal."

Hadina felt the tears roll down her face as she looked at her little sister. She looked so much like their mother that sometimes it took Hadina's breath away. But it also meant that she always had a reminder of her *Mami* whenever she needed it.

"God, I miss *Mami*. She always knew exactly what to do or what to say."

"No, she didn't. You and Zellie think that she was a Saint, but she was human. And yes, she was the absolute best person, but don't put her up on a pedestal like that. Our humanity and mistakes is what makes us strong. Our flaws and our faults are what we learn from. *Mami* learned from hers so that she could teach us to be better. So that her daughters knew family mattered most."

"You're so smart, Piper."

Piper rolled her eyes and smacked Hadina with the pillow she was holding. "Yes, I am. You should listen to me more often."

Hadina smiled. "I think I can manage that."

"We'll find her, Hadi. But we'll do it as a family. Just like *Mami* would have wanted."

CHAPTER 4

PEYTON HAD NO IDEA HOW LONG IT HAD BEEN SINCE SHE'D BEEN TAKEN but she figured it must've been days at the least. Her head throbbed and she struggled to open her eyes against the low light of the room. Her right eye was almost completely swollen shut and she winced as the movement disturbed the wounds on her face.

Wounds courtesy of the woman who had given her life.

Her entire body was in burning agony every time she breathed. Peyton was almost positive that Old Smokey and his crony had broken a few of her ribs when they decided to practice kickboxing on her already tortured body. Demi had started with simply beating her, berating her as she did so. But then she invited her dutiful employees to take their best shot and, well...they hit bullseye more than once.

The tears she'd cried to begin with were now long gone, dried up at the same time she realized she would have to shut her heart off if she wanted to survive.

And she *would* survive. She would make her way back to Hadina and curse the woman for ever letting her leave.

God, she missed her. She was so angry at Hadina for not following her that night. Her anger was misplaced, she knew, but it was easier to be angry than to face any of the other emotions she was feeling. Her heart hurt more than the physical pain she was in, and she didn't have enough energy to analyze that.

"You know, it's really a shame that you appeared back in my life. I'd happily torture anyone who was useful, but it's extra rewarding for me that I can kill two birds with one stone: hurt Hadina Adis, and get rid of you at the same time. If only I could kill you quickly and get it over with."

Peyton let out a low groan through her dry, cracked lips as Demi walked into the room and took a seat in front of her. She was brandishing a knife, holding it up in front of her face for the blade to catch the light. Peyton swallowed thickly as she took in the serrated edge, knowing the weapon was about to tear up her skin.

"What, you don't have anything to say? Don't wanna beg me to stop hurting you?"

"I don't beg," Peyton croaked out, her voice hoarse from screaming, "especially not for scum like you."

Demi smiled and tapped the knife against her pursed lips. "Oh, keep talking like that. It gives me some extra fuel for what I'm about to do to you."

"You know, it's hard for me to believe that anyone was ever capable of putting up with you long enough to even get you pregnant. Did you convince Isaac that you were an angel or something?"

Peyton noted the way Demi's eyes darkened at the mention of her former lover. She was absolutely sure that Demi had felt *something* for him, but Peyton highly doubted it was anything resembling love.

"Isaac was a means to an end. He got what he wanted out of our little dalliance."

"He *died* because of you."

"Lots of people have died at my hand or because of something I did. Isaac knew who I was and he continued to make the decisions he did. I'm not going to feel guilty because of the choices he made."

"You're a heartless bitch," Peyton hissed, flinching when her lip burst open again.

"Oh darling, you have no idea. Remember how I said I was going to break you?" Peyton stared ahead as Demi continued talking, not waiting for a response. "Let me tell you something that I know will help get this process along."

Demi crossed her legs, flipping the handle of the knife between her fingers. Peyton watched her, a loud pounding in her head as she waited for whatever fucked up revelation Demi was about to drop.

"A few years ago, Zellie Adis came to see me. She wanted to work together, she said. But the thing about the Adis family is that they all think they're so fucking smart. She clearly hadn't done her research properly, otherwise she'd have known that I knew her *Papi* and that he'd never agree to work with me. Especially not considering the last time I'd seen him, he was giving me a duffle bag of money to make sure I never contacted you again."

Peyton felt her jaw slacken as she gawped at Demi. "*You* were who Zellie wanted to work with?! Why?"

"Because she loves money and power almost as much as I do," Demi laughed, rolling her eyes as though the answer was obvious. "But the thing is, I don't want or need to work *with* people. If Adis & Co. was so weak that they wanted to work with me, it meant they were weak enough for me to take over."

"So what happened?" Peyton asked, hating how lost in the dark she felt.

"Zellie didn't take my rejection well. Like I said, she thought she was so smart to come to me, but instead she'd just shown her weakness. When I told her I'd take their company for myself, she thought she'd threaten me."

A dry laugh escaped Peyton's lips. "You're too selfish to have leverage for anyone to hold over you. What, did she tell you she was going to kill your puppy or something?"

Demi looked at her with disgust and disappointment, shaking her head. She ran one of her perfectly manicured fingers down the edge of the blade, almost like a loving caress.

"Silly girl. *Everyone* has something that can be used as leverage... She had found out about you."

"I-uh-what?"

She sighed and leveled her gaze at Peyton. "Little Adis thought she would use you to bargain with me. That she'd discovered some conspiracy and that I had given you away because of some foolish maternal instinct." The revulsion in her voice was thick as she spoke. Demi Treyva was not born to be a mother. "Unluckily for her, I didn't give a flying fuck what happened to you. But she made one mistake."

Peyton felt trepidation walk down her spine. "And what mistake was that? This is an awfully long story time and I'm starting to get bored."

"She told me where you were. When I made that agreement with Don, I really didn't care if I was ever going to see you again. He wanted to protect Isaac's legacy; I wanted to get rid of my mistake. Everything was fine if I never heard anything about you ever again. But then fucking Zellie thought she could use you as some sort of bargaining chip over me? I couldn't let that happen again."

Her stomach churned as Peyton listened, an unsettling feeling coursing through her blood. She watched Demi, unfeeling and crazy, and knew that whatever she told her next was going to be far worse than she could have imagined.

"What did you do?"

Demi sucked her teeth, tilting her head to look at Peyton. "You know, you really did look eerily alike. You and Melina—that was your sister's name, right?"

"No! You don't get to talk about her. Don't you say her name!"

Demi's answering cackle filled the air. "*Melina, Melina, Melina.* The stupid girl wasn't supposed to be home. My men were on strict instructions on what to do, had even studied images of you so they knew who they were going after. But when they got to your house, it was your sister who was home. You were too busy yapping to one of your little friends and came home late..."

"No, no, no," Peyton whispered to herself, shaking her head. Demi was making this up—she had to be.

"It's your own fault really. You were late; how were my men to know? They saw dear little Melina who looked just like the girl they'd seen and they did what they were being paid to do."

"NO!" Peyton screamed, thrashing against the ropes holding her down. "I found her. She'd done it herself. I waded through the bloody water myself!"

Demi stood, pushing her chair back as she towered over Peyton. Leaning down, she pressed her lips close to Peyton's ear so that she could whisper. "My men covered her mouth with a chloroform rag, ignoring her screams until she passed out. And then they filled the bathtub with her in it, before they took razors to her wrists and made it look like a suicide. Your perfect little Melina didn't kill herself, Peyton. *I* killed her...but it was supposed to be you."

Bile rose up in chunks in the back of Peyton's throat and she vomited down herself, watching as it splattered onto Demi's perfect yellow blouse. She sobbed as she continued to puke, the nightmare images of her sister's lifeless body morphing into scenes of murder.

CHAPTER 5

Hadina - one week later

Hadina grabbed the bottle of tequila and poured herself another shot. Her head was pounding and the only thing helping to quiet her mind was the bitter burn of alcohol. She had never been one for drinking but if she would allow herself to be drunk over anything, it was the fuckshow of her life right now.

She looked around her for something to chase the tequila with but came up with nothing. There was probably soda in the kitchen, but she didn't want to move from her stupor. She had been sitting on the floor behind her desk for a few hours, curled up in herself like a baby. Thinking hurt her head and her heart, so it was better to be drunk and have her thoughts inhibited.

Fury roared in her veins if she allowed herself even a second to think. Hadina was consumed with worry for Peyton, anger at her team for not having found her yet, and also rage at Demi. She wanted to find that woman and rip her apart limb by limb. But mostly, Hadina was furious at herself. She should have followed Peyton when she ran from the house, should have made sure that she was okay.

It was her job to protect Peyton, and she had failed.

She had let Peyton down.

Another shot.

"Regresa a mí, tentadora," she whispered into the now-empty bottle. She let a couple of tears fall free, unable to find the willpower to hold them back anymore.

God, when was the last time she had felt so lost, so broken?

When her *Mami* had passed away.

Losing her had broken the entire family and the only thing that kept them together was the broken parts of each other. But now it felt like she was broken on her own, and she was cutting herself open on the broken parts of herself that never healed from the first heartbreak.

A sob tore free and Hadina grabbed the empty bottle, throwing it against the wall with an almighty scream. The glass shattered everywhere and she let out a hoarse laugh, feeling defeated as she looked at the mess.

Curling her arms around herself, she sat up and looked towards the framed photo of her mother. She looked so beautiful and happy in the snapshot, her smile bright and her hazel eyes glistening in the sunlight. Her dark hair was down in loose curls around her shoulder, not unlike how Hadina chose to wear hers often.

Hadina had loved her mother more than anyone and the loss of her felt just as raw every day. The absence of her in their lives was so apparent in everything they did. She'd think of something funny and want to share it with her *Mami*, only to have the horrifying realization that she couldn't. Even after all these years had passed, it never got easier.

"I wanted to be good for her, *Mami,* but I let her down," she said on a soft cry, staring at the photo. "I wanted to be good for you, too. But I do bad things and God is coming to collect payment for my sins. Maybe this pain is what I get. Is God punishing me? I'll take it if He is, *Mami,* but I just need to know she's okay. I need her to be safe, even if it means I have to live life without her afterwards."

Tears flooded down her cheeks as she spoke to her mother, wishing more than anything that she could hear her voice. She scrunched her eyes closed and let herself feel *everything,* roaring in an agonizing scream as she thudded her fists on the carpeted floor. She pounded her fists until she felt her skin break, specks of blood smearing onto the carpet.

At some point, unconsciousness pulled her under but even sleep haunted Hadina with thoughts of her beloved mother and her missing lover.

IT HAD BEEN OVER A WEEK SINCE PEYTON HAD BEEN KIDNAPPED AND Hadina's team still couldn't find her. They were trying everything —because they'd have to face Hadina's wrath if they didn't—and yet there was no sign of her. Demi hadn't surfaced and it made Hadina's skin itch. The more worried she became, the looser her grip on reality became.

The stoic, collected *reina de las sombras* was allowing herself to become insanity incarnate. But she didn't care... Hadina would make a deal with *el diablo* if it meant she could save Peyton.

In fact, that was a gross understatement. Hadina would *become* the devil and wreak havoc on the world if Peyton wasn't returned to her.

Loneliness was a dangerous thing and could make even the

sanest person go mad. Even surrounded by her family who were rallying to help her, Hadina had never felt so lonely. Peyton had forced her way inside, invading her every sense and latching onto her soul; without her, life felt pointless.

Sitting at her desk, Hadina looked at the mess of her office. At some point, she'd woken and made her way to the kitchen. A plate of *enchiladas* sat covered on the kitchen island, a note from her father stuck on top telling her to eat. She'd contemplated eating them but chose to stick to her liquid diet.

The copious amounts of tequila had her feeling numb, yet she became more erratic the more she drank. From the looks of the mess, she had trashed the entire office at some point in a fit of rage. Now joining the broken bottle, books were discarded across the floor, chairs upturned, paper strewn everywhere.

"*Mierda,*" she whispered to herself as she stood, staggering slightly. She ran a hand through her hair, groaning when she found her curls had become matted strands from neglect. Her mouth felt dry and the taste of tequila lingered on her lips, making her feel nauseous as she remembered the burning feeling.

Hadina stepped around the desk, tiptoeing across the carpet to avoid standing on the broken glass. As she opened the door, the scent of eggs being fried wafted through the house. The nausea she had been feeling rose up the back of her throat and she had barely made it a step before she vomited onto the wooden flooring of the hallway. As she emptied her guts, Hadina slid to her knees, her stomach and throat burning.

"God, you look like shit," Harris said from behind her, walking around the pile of vomit to help her stand.

Wiping her mouth with the back of her hand, Hadina shrugged off his helping hands and offered only a glare in return. "What are you even doing here? I didn't tell you to come over here this morning."

Harris shook his head, looking at her with pity which made her blood boil. "Morning? Hadina, it's just gone three in the afternoon. You've been passed out in a drunken stupor!" Realizing who he had raised his voice to, Harris adjusted his tone. "Your sister asked me to come over because she's worried about you. Piper figured I could talk some sense into you, or at the very least you'd let me close enough to make sure you were okay."

"I don't need a fucking babysitter, Adrian," Hadina snapped, starting to walk away from him. "Piper worries over nothing."

"I wouldn't call *this*," Adrian waved his hand in the air, gesturing to her appearance, "nothing. You're clearly not coping."

"I'm perfectly fine."

"Hadina, we can't find Peyton and if we have any hope of finding her—"

"I need to be on top of my game. I heard you the last fifty times. I know what I'm doing. *¡No olvides quién es la jefa!*"

Harris continued to talk but Hadina was done listening. She needed fresh air and to get away from the stifling concern of her family. She didn't want to be mad at them just because they cared, but it was pissing her off the way they were watching her like she was a bomb waiting to blow.

Her father was the worst of them all. He felt so guilty that he was smothering her, constantly hovering around and apologizing over and over. Apologies didn't make it better and it sure as fuck didn't bring Peyton back to her. She needed space if he wanted forgiveness and even then, forgiveness was not hers to give.

Besides, his betrayal hurt worse than anything else. He had always preached about the importance of honesty and communication; family didn't hide behind half truths and buried secrets. They had enough skeletons in their closet—almost literally, which really didn't make it any better—so his lies cut deep. Hadina would have understood and she would have found a way to tell

Peyton without causing the heartbreak and devastation that the girl had suffered.

But he hadn't given her that opportunity.

Hadina breathed a sigh of relief as she got out the front door, filling her lungs with the crisp air. She looked down at her bare feet and groaned, knowing she would only cut up her soles if she tried to walk down the graveled pathway. Remembering she had some spare shoes in the back of her car, Hadina crept inside to grab her keys and then made her way to retrieve the shoes.

"Gotcha!" she muttered as she found the pair of black running shoes in the trunk. While she had mastered the art of living in high heels and stilettos, Hadina knew there would always be times where she needed to run and not be caught; running shoes would only aid her when that happened.

She quickly pulled the shoes onto her bare feet and then walked back to the front of the house, taking a seat on the step. A quick text to her team had a driver picking her up within ten minutes in a sleek black Cadillac, ready to take her wherever she wanted to go.

Honestly, she had no idea where she wanted to go. If she was being rational, she knew she looked a mess and stank of alcohol, so she definitely wasn't going to show her face in public.

She could go to her apartment, but she had taken Peyton there before and it would remind her of what she was missing.

Kaira would welcome her without too much criticism, but she'd want Hadina to discuss her feelings, which was the last thing she wanted to do.

Hadina was in pain and she was drowning. She had been drowning for a long time, but Peyton had come into her life and kept her afloat. Without her, she was slowly sinking to depths she couldn't come back from.

A thought occurred to Hadina and she threw her head back against the seat as she contemplated whether she was really going to do it. The pulling feeling in her gut was the thing telling her that it was what she needed to do, even if that was the last place she wanted to go.

Leaning forward, she gave the driver the address on where to go and then relaxed into her seat. She needed to preserve her energy.

SHE TOLD THE DRIVER TO LEAVE HER—SHE'D CALL IF SHE NEEDED TO BE picked up—but her feet wouldn't move from their spot on the sidewalk. Hadina stared up at the old factory building and cursed herself for even considering showing up here.

Forcing herself forward, Hadina made her way around to the back of the building which was now used as the entrance. Sliding the metal door aside, Hadina stepped into the building and stood in the foyer.

It had been a long time since she'd been here and she couldn't help but stare in awe of the beautiful interior. While the outside looked old and abandoned, it was definitely by design. Inside had been remodeled completely, although the industrial look had been kept. Exposed brick walls, metal beams low hanging from the ceiling, old ventilation systems polished but still attached to the walls; it was truly stunning in its simplicity.

"*¿Que demonios estas haciendo aquí?*"

Hadina straightened her back and steeled herself as she turned around to look at her sister. "*Hola, hermana.*"

Zellie rolled her eyes and stepped aside, motioning for Hadina to enter. Hadina followed her sister as she led her through more of the building and into a small side room she had renovated into a sitting area. It was minimalistic with a low, black leather sofa and matching armchairs. A long, oval coffee table sat in the middle of the room, a few magazines and controllers for the flatscreen TV—which was mounted onto the brick wall—littered on top.

Hadina watched as Zellie lit a cigarette, taking a seat on the armchair furthest from her. She crossed one leg across the other, her wide leg pants rising to expose the small knife tucked into her boots.

"Well, to what do I owe the pleasure, Hadina?"

"Maybe I've come to make you face the consequences of what you did to Harris."

Zellie barked out a laugh. "*Hermana*, you don't have any weapons on you. You think I'm not able to recognise when someone *isn't* strapped up? Besides, you look like shit and you absolutely reek of alcohol. *Eres un desastre.*"

"You're right. I don't have weapons on me and honestly Adrian's wound is the last thing on my mind. But you know that, don't you?"

She watched as her big sister evaluated her, taking a long draw of her cigarette before nodding. "I've spoken to Piper. She had a few choice words for me, but we both know she's a kitty cat. She yelled at me, cried, yelled some more... She's been calling me every day since with some updates."

Piper's heart was what made her so special, so kind, but her ability to forgive and move on was something Hadina would never be able to understand. No matter what Zellie said or did, Piper always gave her a free pass.

"*¿Qué deseas?* Why are you really here, Hadina?"

Hadina considered Zellie, watching her as she sat stoically, puffing on her cigarette in slow, deliberate actions. While they'd always had a difficult relationship, Hadina remembered how much she used to love and dote on her big sister. She had spent years trying to be someone like her, until she realized that Zelina was simply a cold, calculating *puta*.

But if anyone understood the way she was hurting inside, it was Zellie.

"I'm here because I need your help."

Zellie raised her eyebrows, not bothering to hide the shock on her face. She stubbed out her cigarette in an ashtray and leaned forward, resting her elbows on her knees. "What could I possibly do to help you?"

"I don't know, but I know that I need all the help I can get." Hadina took a deep breath, running her hands through her hair. She could feel the grease on the strands and she made a mental note to shower when she got home. It had been longer than she cared to admit. "All I know is that Peyton is out there somewhere and I can't find her on my own. And the longer time goes on, the worse it's getting for her. You helped Demi get free—this is on you. You *owe* me this."

"I don't owe you shit, Hadina."

Emotions began to swirl in her chest and whether it was the lack of control over herself or the lowered inhibitions from a night of drinking, Hadina found herself unable to push them down. A sob broke free and she buried her face in her hands. She was ashamed that of all the people to see her like this, it was Zellie.

"Fine! You don't owe me. But however you want to look at this, you helped Demi and then she kidnapped Peyton."

"Why does this girl matter so much to you? *El amor te ha hecho débil.*"

Hadina shook her head, looking up at Zellie through her tears. "Love has not made me weak! She matters because she is *everything good* about this world—especially the fucked up world we reside in. We spend our lives in the darkness, Zelina; Peyton is the light keeping me from disappearing completely."

Zellie was silent for a moment. "I don't remember the last time I saw you cry."

"Yes, you do. Because it was the last time I saw you cry, too."

"When *Mami* died."

Hadina nodded, using the sleeve of her shirt to wipe her face. "I have barely felt anything since *Mami* died. And then Peyton turned up at the house and my whole fucking world changed. *Este dolor hace que me duela el corazón de la misma manera que lo hizo perder a Mami.* I can't lose her. I can't go through that pain again. I will not survive it."

"*Entiendo. Yo te ayudo,*" Zellie said, her voice uncharacteristically quiet. "But first, there's something you need to know."

CHAPTER 6

HADINA

HADINA WATCHED HER SISTER—THE PERSON WHO HAD TAUGHT HER HOW to be calm and collected—fidget nervously and chew on her lower lip. Just the thought of Zellie being nervous made *her* feel uneasy. Which was deeply annoying because Hadina was already feeling far too much.

"*Entonces habla.* What is it you have to tell me?"

Zelina brushed a strand of her short hair behind her ear, her hand almost trembling, something the untrained eye wouldn't have caught. But Hadina was more than trained and could spot a myriad of things in the human behavior.

"I made a mistake...a big one. When *Papi* first stepped down from Adis & Co. and put me in charge, I was looking through a bunch of the documents and trying to store things in a more efficient way. But I found something and when I confronted him, he told me everything."

Hadina narrowed her eyes. "You knew, didn't you? You found the birth certificate."

Zellie nodded. "I was confused at first. I wanted to know why *Papi* had it in his possession. At first, I foolishly thought it was some illegitimate sibling we didn't know about. I saw the fear in his eyes when I waved it in his face."

"What did you do, Zelina?"

"Well, you know most of the story. I figured we should work with some of our *opposition* if we really wanted to go after the sick bastards we do. You and I both know that there are many more people we can't reach; people not within our circles. Demi's circle would give us an in."

It took all of her willpower for Hadina to bury her growl and sit still. Zellie had split their family apart when she tried to make those connections, work with those disgusting people. Demi Treyva was scum. She'd push drugs, booze, bodies...whatever it took to make money. Hadina still harbored hate for her sister for betraying their code like that.

"That's not what we stand for, though. *Protegemos a los inocentes.* Demi is everything we stand against. You should have known better."

Zellie looked up at the ceiling, blowing out a long breath. "I got greedy, okay? Is that what you want to hear? I know I messed up. I thought I could do a better job than *Papi* and that I could make him proud of me if I could go after bigger targets. In my mind, Demi was simply a means to an end."

Despite her anger, Hadina could partially understand where her sister was coming from. Zellie was an asshole, but her heart beat with the same purpose that Hadina's did: save the people who couldn't save themselves. Zellie had gone about it all wrong, but her reason for doing so made sense.

"*¿Entonces qué pasó?*"

"*Papi* omitted some of the vital details about Demi. Like the fact he had *paid her* to give Peyton up for adoption. I thought she was just a screwed up woman who made a series of bad choices. I figured I could use Peyton as leverage. *Papi* had all the details about where she was and her adoptive family..."

"*Mierda*," Hadina cursed, rubbing her temples. "Tell me you weren't that fucking naïve, Zellie."

"I know how stupid it was! But it didn't seem like such a bad idea at the time. I arranged a meeting and told her I knew about Peyton. I told her I knew where she was, what she looked like. Then this *perra psicótica* laughed like I had told her the funniest joke in the world. She said she didn't care where Peyton was."

Hadina shook her head, gripping onto the armrests of her chair to stop her finding something to throw at her sister. "But you couldn't let it go, could you?"

Zellie threw up her hands. "Of course I couldn't! What kind of *pinche puta* acts like that? We were raised by *Mami*, Hadina—I couldn't fathom someone *not* loving their child when *Mami* loved us so fiercely."

She was taken aback by that admission from Zellie and it struck Hadina in her heart. While she could be angry with Zellie for the stupidity of her actions, she also would never be able to comprehend why Demi was so heartless. Their mother had showed them love at every moment of their lives and losing her was something they could never recover from. And Demi had simply given away her opportunity to have that connection. She understood why people gave children up for adoption—she wasn't stupid—but Demi didn't have a *reason* for doing it. No reason other than greed and wanting.

"I threatened her, Hadina," Zellie whispered solemnly. "I threatened Peyton's life when Demi refused to work with me. I thought I could force her hand.

"It was like a switch flicked in her. She laughed like a fucking maniac, called me a stupid little girl, and told me to leave. I know when I've lost and I refused to dignify her with me arguing like a schoolgirl."

Things started to slot in place for Hadina as Zellie continued talking. The alcohol in her stomach was threatening to come back up and she had to focus on a point on the wall to stop the room from spinning around her. She wished she hadn't come here, especially not when she was still half drunk and dizzy. She no longer wanted to know any of this information.

"I... Demi was beyond pissed that I thought I could use Peyton as leverage over her. Instead of finding a way to protect her daughter, she decided it was better to just get rid of her so nobody could ever assume she had a weakness."

Hadina rose to her feet and began pacing the living room, suddenly wishing that she had stayed home and found another bottle of tequila to drown her sorrows with.

"Stop, please. I don't think I can hear anymore right now."

Zellie stood too, stepping closer to Hadina. "You have to hear it, Hadi. I have to *say* it. Demi sent people to kill Peyton but they messed up. I don't know if the girl's ever shown you photos of her sister, but they could have almost passed as twins. Peyton was running late on the day Demi's men arrived, but her sister Melina was at home. They murdered that poor girl and staged a suicide."

"You stupid fool!" Hadina yelled, stepping away from Zellie. "Her blood is on your hands. You know that Peyton was the one to find her, right? She's traumatized for life because of *your* fuck up!"

For the first time in years, Hadina watched her sister's eyes fill with tears. "I know that! I told *Papi* straight away and I begged him to do something. It's why he started paying for her schooling; why he even hired her to work for you guys in the first place."

Hadina thought back to the sadness that seeped out of Peyton from the moment she stepped foot at the house. She remembered the absolute heartbreak in her voice as she told Hadina about her sister, about the way it had devastated her life.

And all this time, it was her own sister's actions which had cost Peyton the one person in life who had loved and protected her.

A violent vehemence filled Hadina's veins and before she knew what she was doing, her fist was connecting with Zellie's nose. She heard the bones crack beneath her hand, blood gushing from her sister's face. Seeing her bleed was like waving a red flag before a bull and all Hadina could think about was making Zellie hurt the way she had made Peyton hurt all these years.

"You took away the one person she had, Zellie. Losing her sister made her empty the way that losing *Mami* made us!" She took another swing, landing this hit to her chin with such force that Zellie stumbled backward, tripping over the coffee table and landing on the floor.

Climbing over her sister, she straddled her hips and landed another two blows to her face. She could barely see Zellie's face now that it was covered in blood, her nose still gushing and her lip split open. "As if that wasn't enough, you fucking let her go to the restaurant with us. You let Demi see her and then you helped that *bastarda* go free! You knew she would come for Peyton and you still helped her!"

"I let her go because I knew she would tell you what had happened, or that she'd tell Peyton the truth. I thought I could get ahead of the game somehow; that I'd let her go and then be able to trap her afterwards. After I shot Adrian, I tried to follow her. I thought I could kill her myself and get it over with."

Hadina roared, pounding her fists against Zellie's chest. She no longer had the energy to fight her, but she couldn't stop wanting to hurt her. Zellie was the direct cause of everything that was going wrong in her life... She was the reason that Hadina may lose the love of her life.

As she went to land another hit, Zellie grabbed her by the wrists and shook her. "*¡Basta!* You came here because you need me; let me do this. *Mami* would want us to get Peyton back safe, and you need me to do it. You can go back to hating me afterwards. Let me correct my fucking wrong, Hadi. Let me do this for you, *mi hermana*."

All the emotions and hurt that Hadina had been trying to bury came flooding out in wracking sobs. She collapsed into Zellie's shoulder, crying uncontrollably. The scene, while far more bloody, reminded her of how she'd similarly collapsed into Zellie when their *Mami* had passed, which only made her hurt more.

Zellie loosened her grip on her wrists and wrapped her arms around Hadina's crying frame. From the small shudder she felt every few seconds, Hadina thought Zellie may have been crying too.

"You think I wanted this to happen? You think I want that kind of blood on my hands? I may be a piece of shit, Hadina, but I'm not like *that*. I have fucked up so much in my life and I'm okay with that because that's my shit, but now that my actions have touched you in the worst way...I can't live with that on my conscience. I can't take it back, but I can help you find Peyton and end this once and for all."

CHAPTER 7

The thing about learning the truth was that it always came at a price. Peyton had begged into the abyss so many times, wishing that her sister would come back to her, wishing that she hadn't chosen to leave her alone. And now that she knew that Melina *hadn't* chosen to take her own life... She couldn't make sense of it in her head. Every thought was an excruciating pain, a dagger to her heart, knowing it should have been her that died.

Her sister had died because of her.

Consciousness was haunting her, playing a twisted game with her. She would wake, only to be beaten and broken some more. She had cried until her whole body became numb. Now she almost welcomed the pain, the physical reminder that she was still alive.

If she was alive, it meant Hadina would still be able to save her.

Hadina.

God, she missed Hadina more than anything. She ached to be

in her arms, feel her lips on her own, to hear that familiar whisper of *tentadora*.

She had no concept of how long it had been since she'd been kidnapped, but it felt like an eternity. With only Demi and her henchmen for company, Peyton was reminded of how it felt to drown in her own loneliness. Hadina Adis had reminded her how it felt to be loved and to matter—without her, existence felt like a torturous waste.

"You know," Old Smokey said as he entered the room, blowing smoke from his cigarette directly into Peyton's face, "I could hurt you real bad and just tell boss lady it was complications from your wounds. Me and my buddy could have some fun."

Old Smokey—who was actually called Reggie, but Peyton couldn't bring herself to humanize him when he was the one dehumanizing *her*—and his counterpart, Pete, had been taking turns to beat the shit out of her until she passed out. They'd leave her unconscious for a little while and then douse her with cold water, waking her just to repeat the process. They got their sick little kicks from watching her live reactions to the pain they caused, hearing her screams.

But Peyton had learned a thing or two from Hadina. Wearing a mask was second nature to Hadi, and Peyton had studied that woman like she was a piece of the finest art.

She would no longer give them the reactions they craved.

Staring at a spot in the wall, Peyton kept her face blank as the two men circled her. She felt Pete run his hands over her shoulders, his dirty fingers slipping lower to fondle her breasts through her torn clothes. It took every bit of willpower she had to not throw her head back and crack his nose, but she was biding her time. Peyton had a plan, but she needed everything to be perfect.

"Look at you. Sitting there with your *fuck me* eyes but not offering us anything. Why don't we just take what we want, Pete? Demi won't be back for a while..."

Peyton closed her eyes and shut out the sound of the men talking, making vulgar comments about what they wanted to do to her body. She felt their hands roaming across her body, one of them ripping at the fabric of her shirt to reveal more of her skin, but she blocked it out. Hadina's face appeared in her mind, that *I don't give a fuck* look on her face. Peyton smiled inwardly and mimicked the expression.

Seeing Hadina, even in her mind's eye, was like igniting a flame inside her. Her plan was to wait until Demi was back, taking over from her henchmen, and Peyton would pick a fight. She felt the chair beneath her groan every so often, so she knew there was a weakness in the wood somewhere. If she could get Demi to hit her hard enough, get the angle just right, she could fall back on the chair with enough force to break it. If that could happen...

But Hadina wouldn't wait. Her beautiful, badass woman had taught her so much in their short time together. Images of the rigorous training Hadina and Harris had made her endure flashed through her head, like a montage to remind her of exactly what she was now capable of. Peyton hadn't just had a few self defense lessons with her girlfriend—no, she had trained how to be a warrior. How to be a part of the Adis & Co. team. Peyton was one of them, and that meant she was capable of far more than she ever had been.

Nobody would ever make her a victim again.

Opening her eyes, Peyton felt herself grinning. She knew that it would be a look of absolute psychosis from the outside, but to her, it was the type of grin that would make Hadina proud. It was the grin of a fucking fighter. Her woman was *la Reina de las sombras*, and she had learned how to command the shadows beside her.

"Look, Reggie, the whore is enjoying that. Aren't ya, doll?"

Peyton tilted her head at Pete, angling it so he could press closer to her. When there was barely any space between them, Peyton brought her head back and swung forward with as much force as possible. A blinding pain traveled through her as the bones of her already broken nose crunched. Pete let out a scream, his filthy hands covering his face as blood gushed from his nose.

"You little bitch!" Old Smokey screamed, grabbing her by the throat.

"I may be a bitch, but at least I don't rape and batter women because I'm too ugly to get any action on my own," Peyton threw back, venom laced in her voice.

Old Smokey squeezed her throat, but a plan was quickly forming in her head. She struggled against him and, just as she had assumed Demi would, Old Smokey hit her with enough anger that she fell backwards. The crack of the weak wood brought a vindictive smile to her face. Her body temporarily eased with newfound freedom.

"Stay down! Pete, grab her legs."

Peyton laughed as the men took position at either end of her. What they didn't know—or simply were too dumb to pay enough attention to see—was the way in which the chair had snapped. Both her hands and legs were now free, for the most part. The spokes of wood that her ropes were tied to still remained bound to her, but that simply gave her leverage. Her hands and feet weren't tied *together* and the assholes hadn't noticed.

Pete kneeled at her feet, grabbing her calves with his meaty hands. Peyton waited a second, biding her time as Old Smokey grabbed her by the hair. She slowly, almost imperceptibly, twisted her wrists to grab hold of the wooden spokes attached to her hands. Once she had a good grip, she waited for her moment.

"I'm going to make you regret ever opening your mouth," Old Smokey ground out, yanking her head back.

"I'd believe you if you weren't just a pathetic excuse of a man," Peyton chuckled. She watched as Old Smokey's eyes filled with hate. He let go of her hair to reach into his pocket for a knife, which was the opportunity she had been waiting for.

With him distracted for a split second, and both of Pete's hands holding down her legs, Peyton took a deep breath and thrust her arm upwards with all the power she had inside her. She held her breath as the wooden spike impaled Old Smokey through the neck. She did her best to block out the way it felt tearing through his skin, or the sound of his bloodied gasp.

"What the FUCK?!" Pete yelled, scrambling to grab her. Peyton kicked at him, slamming her foot into his face. She rolled over and stuck her hand into Old Smokey's pocket, cursing as his blood coated her hands. He let out a spluttering groan, but Peyton focused and steadied herself.

She caught hold of the knife just as Pete grabbed hold of her hips, flipping her over. Peyton used the momentum to flick the blade open, driving it upwards. Pete cursed and looked down with widened eyes, staring at the place Peyton had just stuck the knife. Not waiting another second, she delivered a second stab, then a third. Fourth. Fifth.

Peyton had no idea how many times she plunged the blade into him. But by the time she had stopped, blood was splattered across her face and chest, smeared across her pale skin. She blinked, coming back to herself, dropping the knife by her side.

She had just killed two men and yet she felt nothing.

Nobody would ever make her a victim again, and she would kill anyone who tried.

Peyton Dimitra was *la tentadora de las sombras* and she needed to find her queen.

CHAPTER 8

SITTING BEHIND HER DESK IN THE ADIS & CO. OFFICE BUILDING FELT LIKE a surreal experience for Hadina. It had been so long since she had come to work for anything other than supplies on her search for Peyton. But now, she sat there and awaited news from her sisters and her team. Being at home had made her go stir crazy and she was itching to drown herself in another bottle of tequila; the only way for her to escape the demons plaguing her was for her to outrun them.

Temporarily, at least.

She looked around the room, the blank walls reflecting her empty heart. Hadina had always thought that keeping the office looking *professional* was all that mattered, but now it just made her feel isolated. Had she really been so alone before Peyton that even her everyday life was nothing but blank walls and bloodshed?

Yes, that was *exactly* how lonely she had been. Maybe it hadn't been clear to her before, but it certainly was now.

Without Peyton, Hadina was drifting in a sea of darkness and she no longer had the energy to command the shadows to keep her afloat. If she didn't find her love soon, she would let herself be consumed.

"*Jefa!* We have a lead!"

The sound of Harris' voice breaking through her cloud of dark thoughts was a welcome relief. Hadina shot out of her chair and practically ran down the corridor and into the tech room. It was technically more of an office section, with more than thirty monitors and a couple of data analysts working, furiously typing at their keyboards.

Harris stood behind one of the analysts, Josie, and beckoned Hadina over. Her sisters were already there, peering at the computer.

"What is it?"

"I think we know where that *pinche panocha* is hiding. There's an old house that used to belong to Isaac's family. When he died, they picked up and moved away, abandoning the house," Zellie explained. "It's right at the edge of the city, crumbling to pieces in the middle of one of the dying forests there."

"Pull up the photos," Hadina commanded. She watched as Josie clicked at her keyboard and pulled up the enlarged images on the screen mounted to the wall above the computer. As soon as she saw the old cottage-style house, Hadina felt a tug in her stomach.

"She's there."

Harris coughed. "We don't know that. We should check it out first."

Zellie looked at her sister and Hadina could see the understanding in her eyes. She didn't know if their relationship was reparable, but Zellie had stepped up and done what she had agreed —she'd been by Hadina's side to aid her in finding Peyton. Her expertise was the missing piece in their search for her girl.

"She's there," Zellie confirmed, nodding her head to Hadina. "If

Hadina has a feeling, we should trust her gut. She knows what she's doing."

It cut Hadina deep to hear those words from her big sister. She had longed for her acceptance and approval for so many years that she'd given up; to hear her give it so freely now was overwhelming.

"It's time to bring my *tentadora* home."

It only took them two hours to come up with their game plan. Hadina went into a fugue state as she ordered her team about, yelling at them to move faster. Both Zellie and Piper were the embodiment of Adis daughters as they stormed through the building, ensuring Hadina's commands were being followed out to perfection.

Harris, however, stayed by Hadina's side. She knew he was apprehensive about them going full on SWAT team without more information and reconnaissance, but Hadina didn't give a flying fuck. She would send her team across the fucking world if it meant she would find Peyton.

She just hoped they reached her in time.

The drive to the outskirts of the city was only ten minutes and yet it felt like hours as Hadina bit at her thumbnail nervously. She needed to focus, but her mind was filled with horrific scenes of what they could be turning up to, what version of Peyton they may find.

"Almost there, *jefa*. Are you ready?" Harris asked quietly from the driver's seat beside her.

Hadina remained silent until they pulled up to the edge of the trees, grateful for the silence of the vehicle. She let out a quick breath and squared her shoulders, throwing a glance at Harris. "I'm always ready."

The teams jumped out of the five parked cars, grabbing their guns and lifting them into position. Hadina nodded at each of them respectively, her eyes lingering on Zellie for just a moment long enough to see the determination in her eyes. If anyone was ready to annihilate whoever stood in their way, it was Zelina.

Hadina led the front of the charge as the teams fanned out around each side, spreading throughout the brush of the trees. She could hear the crunch of twigs beneath their heavy footsteps but she forced herself to concentrate on only her own steady steps as she progressed.

A twinge of unfamiliar panic hit her gut as the decrepit cottage came into view. It looked like something from a horror scene, with its dilapidated roof and busted up windows. Planks of rotting wood covered some, though she could see that time had weakened their hold. Overgrown weeds tangled around their ankles and Hadina cursed at them.

The hair on her arms stood tall as a bloodcurdling scream broke through the air. She felt goosebumps cover her entire body and before she could even think, she had taken off in a sprint towards the building. She didn't care that her thumping steps would alert anyone inside, or that Harris and Zellie were both calling to her to wait.

She burst through the front door, following the sound of Peyton's screams. She had her gun poised and the safety off, ready to shoot everyone who tried to stop her from saving her girl. Turning the corner, she stopped dead in her tracks, her eyes widening at the scene before her.

Hadina heard Harris and Zellie coming through the door to stand behind her but she couldn't bring herself to look at them. She couldn't take her eyes off Peyton before her.

Alive.

Broken.

Her beautiful, gentle love was broken.

Screaming, Peyton brought the blade down on the man in front of her, a dead body already on her other side. It was obvious to Hadina that both males were already dead, but still Peyton thrust her knife into him, again and again. Blood covered every inch of her, coating her blonde hair in sticky red clumps.

Hadina's body wouldn't allow her to move. She knew Zellie and Harris were standing by, waiting on her orders, but she didn't have any orders to make. They had found Peyton and yet...

This was her fault. Hadina had given into temptation and allowed herself to wish for Peyton to be part of her life. But *this* was her life. Bloodshed, a trail of dead bodies, and fucking *misery*.

Peyton finally slumped, dropping the blade to her side. Her screams died into sobs as she collapsed to her knees, burying her face in her hands. Hearing the sound of her crying broke whatever trance Hadina was in and she rushed forward, ready to take whatever pain she could from Peyton.

"*Tentadora...* It's me, *mi amor*."

Peyton turned to look at her and Hadina could see her heart physically break in those big blue eyes. "Hadi?"

Without waiting another second, Hadina bundled Peyton in her arms and held the love of her life as she fell to pieces in her embrace. At some point, Hadina's own tears had begun to fall too, but she didn't much care what anyone thought about seeing her weakness. If showing tender parts of herself allowed Peyton to feel stronger and comforted, Hadina would let the vultures eat her.

She didn't know how long passed before Peyton pulled away, looking into her eyes. "You came for me," she whispered tearfully.

Hadina felt an ache in her heart. "Of course I did. *Te seguiría al inframundo, mi amor.* I will always come for you."

"Hadina, we need to go."

Hearing another voice had Peyton flinching into herself. Hadina watched as her eyes turned from scared to something else entirely the moment she saw Zellie standing in the doorway. Hadina had never seen a look of genuine hatred cross Peyton's face, but she was almost sure that's what it was.

"What the fuck are you doing here?!" Peyton yelled, glaring at Zellie.

"*Tentadora*, it's okay. She—Zelina helped me find you."

Peyton turned to Hadina, her face scrunched in horror. "How could you? She *helped* Demi!"

Hadina shook her head. "No, love. It's more complicated than you think. I can explain…"

"NO! I don't want to fucking hear any excuses."

Before Hadina had even registered what was happening, Peyton lurched forward, sprinting directly at Zellie. A moment too late, she saw the blade in her hand as she lunged, swiping it in an arc. The knife cut a sharp line through Zelina's cheek, causing her to cry out and jump out of Peyton's reach.

"This is because of you! If you hadn't let that psycho go, this wouldn't have happened!" Peyton screeched, launching herself in Zellie's direction again.

"*Tentadora*, stop!"

Hadina jumped to her feet and grabbed Peyton by the waist, holding the woman tight against her as she thrashed. "Fucking let me go, Hadina!"

Harris stepped in front of them, a syringe in his hand. Hadina shook her head and batted his hand away but he gripped Peyton by the shoulder, smiling apologetically. "Sorry, P. I gotta do this."

"Don't touch her, Adrian!"

Harris sighed, sticking the plunger into the side of Peyton's neck. "It needs to be done, boss. She has to calm down in order to heal. And we need to get the fuck out of here before Demi comes back."

Hadina looked down at Peyton as her body slumped, her eyes drifting closed. She couldn't help but feel the sting of her own betrayal as Peyton slipped into unconsciousness, knowing that she was the cause of all this pain.

She'd promised to protect Peyton and she had let her down.

Hadina Adis wasn't a queen; she was a monster and she had broken the only person she had ever truly loved.

CHAPTER 9

PEYTON

Rough hands grasped at her body, making nausea roll through her in disgusted waves. They touched her as they pleased, taking what they wanted and laughing at her protests. Bruises marred her skin and blood coated every inch of her.

"Stop!" More laughter echoed as she begged for a reprieve, tears streaming down her pretty face.

"I said fucking *stop!*" she screamed, whipping her arm around her. Suddenly there was a blade in her grip, slicing through the skin of her abusers.

She watched as they bled out, a vindictive smile spreading across her face. She had got her revenge, after all. And it felt *so fucking powerful...*

Peyton woke with a start, her breath coming out in loud gasps as she gulped in air. That dream—nightmare—was so real. She could still feel the unwanted touches and the sticky feeling of fresh blood on her skin.

It took her a moment before reality smacked into her with an unnecessary level of cruelty. Memories overtook her, reminding her of everything she had been through—everything she had done.

A new level of nausea bubbled in her stomach and she turned onto her side, vomiting over the edge of the bed she was in.

She had *killed* people.

Worse, she had *enjoyed* killing them.

Peyton didn't know who she was anymore.

Once the nausea subsided, she rolled onto her back again and looked around the room. At first she thought she was back home in Willowbrooks before she realized that no, she was somewhere else entirely.

She was in Hadina Adis' bed.

"*Tentadora*, you're awake," a familiar voice said from the doorway.

Peyton twisted her head to see Hadina standing in all her goddess-like glory, her long raven hair hanging in straightened strands and giving the appearance of Death itself. It pained Peyton how much her body still craved the woman before her, how her stomach fluttered with childlike innocence at the sight of such pretty features and that dark smile.

But things had changed.

After missing Hadina the entire time she was being held captive, wishing for her sinful kisses and suffocating embraces, Peyton couldn't let herself give in to her foolish feelings. She had been naïve to think that she belonged in this life; that Hadina Adis could be trusted.

No, Hadina was a snake and it was only a matter of time before she unhinged her jaw and devoured Peyton entirely.

"I don't want to see you."

Hadina smirked, shrugging her shoulders as she took a step into the room. "I'm not good at following someone else's orders, darling."

Peyton glared at her, pulling herself up to a sitting position slowly. "You forgave Zellie. You brought her with you to *save me*. I'm not your darling, Hadina. I'm not anything to you anymore."

Tutting, Hadina shook her head and sat at the edge of the bed, making sure to leave space between them. "It's complicated. Forgiveness is a fickle thing and it will take far more than time to make me let my sister off the hook for all the shit she's done. But she helped me find you; I'd be a fool to shun her after that."

"Ha," Peyton said, chuckling dryly, "and here I thought I was the delusional one. Your sister is an evil bitch and you're suddenly teamed up with her? Everything that happened to me... Zellie is the cause of all of this. I won't forgive her just because you think she's repented or some shit."

Hadina closed her eyes and Peyton cursed herself for how much she wanted to lean forward and press her lips against Hadina's painted ones.

"There's more to tell you, *tentadora*. I–I found out a lot of things while you were gone. But you should heal more and then we can talk. I'll tell you everything."

Peyton scoffed, wincing as her stomach muscles contracted. "I don't care, Hadina. The second I don't feel like my body is about to crumble, I'm out of here. I'm done with you and your family and all the fucking secrets. I don't want this."

"You're not leaving," Hadina said dryly. "I will not let you go alone into the world and risk someone else taking you. Risk that *puta* getting her hands on you. I will chain you up and let you hate me forever if I have to, but I *will* protect you. I let you down before —I should never have let you run off on your own. That mistake shall not be repeated."

The devotion and heartache in Hadina's voice was almost enough to break Peyton, but she wouldn't let anything crumble her resolve. She had spent weeks being broken and abused; it was time for her to be her own champion.

"Try it, Hadina. Just try and keep me prisoner. I'll never let someone be my captor again." Tears slipped down her cheeks, burning her already sore skin. "I wanted nothing more than for you to come and save me. You know, I would close my eyes and think about how it felt to be yours; how your tender kisses and rough touches made me feel. Memories and visions of you were what kept me going."

"*Mi amor*," Hadina whispered, reaching out to take Peyton's hand. Peyton flinched and pulled away from her touch, tears falling harder as she gulped.

"I wanted you to save me, Hadina. But you didn't. You left me with them for *weeks* while I was beaten and berated. No matter how much I prayed for you to come find me, you didn't come. I had to wait, to force myself to be strong. You didn't want me to belong in this life of crime you have, but your family is the reason I had to change, had to become someone else. *You didn't save me in time.*"

"I tried!" Hadina stood, making her way around the bed to kneel beside Peyton, careful to avoid the puddle of vomit. "I looked for you, I swear. You never left my mind, Peyton. I did everything I could."

Peyton wiped her face with the back of her hands, sniffing and willing her tears to stop.

"You didn't try hard enough, then. Because I had to become the monster you didn't want me to be. You command your shadows and now I command mine. The darkness belongs to me as much as it does you, and I hate you for it. I love you—more than I ever thought possible—and it makes me so angry that you've twisted my love into something else."

Hadina flinched at the brutality of Peyton's words, rocking back on her heels as though she had physically wounded her. "Please, don't say that. I can handle you hating me, but please don't think I didn't try."

"You call yourself the fucking queen of the shadows! If it took you so long to come for me, then I know you didn't try hard enough. You wrapped yourself up in self pity, while I was being wrapped up in rope. I am the monster in my own nightmares and I will never be able to escape that."

"You're no monster," Hadina pleaded, her eyes watering with her own tears. "You can come back from this, *tentadora*."

Peyton laughed until it turned into strangled sobs, her eyes and nose burning in the process. "There is no coming back from this, Hadi—not for me, not for *us*. I don't need you to teach me how to devour the world; I taught myself. So, go back to your sister and play house and make amends. Leave me to heal and pick up the broken pieces of myself so that I can leave this hell on earth and never come back."

"*Tentadora*, I beg you, *please!*" Hadina whispered. "Don't do this."

"Leave, Hadina. Go back to your kingdom and find someone else to play with. I'm done with tempting you... I'm done with anything the Adis family has to offer."

Hadina bit down on her lip and stood, unblinking and unwilling to look at Peyton. "As you wish."

Peyton watched as the love of her life turned on her heels and followed direction for the first time in her life. Only when the door clicked shut behind her did she allow herself to shatter completely, emotion flooding her system like a tidal wave. She didn't regret a single word she had said, but it didn't make it hurt any less.

The price of betrayal was a bitterness in her heart that she didn't think she would ever be able to escape.

CHAPTER 10

HADINA

As soon as she closed the door behind her, Hadina fell to her knees and allowed herself to sob. She hated this. Hated herself. Peyton was right; this was all her fault and there was no denying that. Even if she wanted to pretend otherwise.

Her stupid actions, Zellie's and her father's too...they had all led to this. Led to heartache and pain for Peyton that she could barely handle. Seeing her heart split in two and the emptiness in her eyes was enough to destroy whatever walls Hadina had left. Her walls were crumbling into dust and so was she.

"*¿Hermana?*"

Hadina looked up to find Piper standing in front of her. She hadn't even heard her approach.

"Hadina? *¿Qué ocurre?* Are you okay?"

"She said she's done," Hadina whispered quietly, her voice broken and sad. "She's done with this family and she...she's done with me, too."

Piper sighed and leaned down, helping to pick Hadina up. "Come. Let's have some tea and you can tell me what she said."

Hadina let her little sister pull her along and into the large sitting area. She sipped from the mug of tea Piper made her, relaying her conversation with Peyton in a monotone voice. She felt empty, like a shell of a human—in pain and all alone.

"*Eres una tonta.* You walked away? Are you freaking dumb?"

Hadina pulled back in shock as though her sister had struck her. Piper was normally so sweet and docile. Though, with everything since Peyton's disappearance, Hadina had noticed a slight change in Piper's demeanor. "She told me to go!"

Piper tutted and shook her head. "Ay, Hadina, I thought you were the smartest of us all! She told you to go because she feels like you didn't try hard enough to fight for her... Leaving again just solidifies that in her mind."

"I won't force myself into her life, *hermana.* She's been through enough."

"*¡Dios mío!* What is wrong with this family and our ability to have healthy communication?"

Hadina rolled her eyes as she looked at her baby sister. "Says the member of this family repressing her feelings."

Piper tensed up and glared at Hadina, crossing her arms over her chest. "I don't know what you're talking about."

"I see the way Adrian looks at you. Don't pretend you don't feel the same."

"Mind your fucking business, Hadi," Piper warned in a tone Hadina knew was usually reserved for Zellie—it hurt her more than she was willing to admit knowing that it was being used on her.

Letting out a sigh, Hadina resigned her argumentative attitude. She chewed nervously at the corner of her lower lip. "You're right. I'm sorry, Pip. I just–I can't handle it if she rejects me again. I love her."

Piper threw her hands up in frustration. "Tell her that! Burying your feelings may have worked for us all our lives, Hadi, but things have changed. You have someone who genuinely *loves you* and you can't afford not to show her that."

Hadina was quiet for a moment before she locked gazes with Piper. "What she went through, what she had to do... I don't know how to help her come back from that, Pip. She said she became a monster and how do I help her when I'm one too?"

"Oh, Hadina," Piper whispered, shaking her head. She stood and made her way to sit next to Hadina, wrapping her arm around her sister's shoulder in comfort. "You're not a monster and neither is Peyton. Calling yourself that is what you've always done to protect yourself and I guarantee it's how Peyton is trying to protect herself too. You have to show her that you love her, darkness and all."

"I do, you know. I love every part of her."

Piper smiled. "I know that, silly. But I'm pretty sure Peyton needs to *hear* those words from you."

Hadina chuckled softly, pulling Piper into a tighter hug. "What would I do without you, little sister?"

"Let's not imagine situations we'll never have to go through, hm?" Piper pulled out of their embrace and pressed a kiss to Hadina's cheek. "Now go win back the heart of your pretty little temptress so that I don't have to find myself a new bestie."

Hadina let herself laugh fully this time. "Yes, ma'am."

⁂

Standing outside the bedroom door, Hadina took a deep breath before knocking lightly.

"Go away," Peyton called out, her voice hoarse from crying.

Hadina waited a moment, debating whether she should come back later after Peyton had had some time to calm down.

No, she thought to herself, *too much time has passed already. That's part of the problem.*

She opened the door and barged inside, closing it behind her. Peyton, who had been curled up in a heap beneath her duvet, sat up in shock and glared at Hadina. "I told you to leave! What are you doing here?"

"I'm not leaving you. Not again."

"I don't want you here," Peyton countered.

Hadina moved to the bottom of the bed, a smirk pulling at her lips. "So make me leave. Tell me you don't love me and I'll go."

"That's not fair and you know it. I told you to leave—why isn't that enough?"

It pained Hadina to hear the hurt and defeat in Peyton's voice, but she wasn't going to give up. She would *never* give up. "Because we both know it isn't what you really want."

Peyton scoffed, swiping her overgrown bangs out of her face. "You barely know me, Hadina. Let's admit that this is more like crazed infatuation and the sooner we cut it off, the better."

"I don't know you, huh?" Hadina repeated, moving around to the edge of the bed. "Funny, because I'd argue that I know you better than anyone. I know the way you *taste*, Peyton. I know how you tremble and bite your lip to stop yourself from screaming when you orgasm." Climbing onto the mattress, Hadina crawled to kneel beside Peyton, looking down at her with a deviousness in her eyes. "I know the way you crave something *more* than the life you've been trapped in. I know that despite everything, the danger associated with my lifestyle gives you a thrill that you want to chase, even if you can't admit it."

Peyton tried not to give a reaction, though Hadina could see from the way her chest rose and fell that she was feeling exactly what Hadina had intended. She was remembering, and her walls were breaking down in the process.

"You think I want to *chase the thrill* after I was just fucking kidnapped?" Peyton snapped. "You're delusional."

A spark ignited in Hadina's core at the violence in Peyton's tone. She knew that it resurfacing meant that *her* Peyton was coming back. Taking a gamble, Hadina hooked one of her legs over Peyton's so that she was straddling her.

"Get off me," Peyton said, though it came out more like a plea, soft and without any confidence.

Hadina trailed her fingertips down Peyton's cheek, reveling in the way Peyton's eyes fluttered at the contact. "I know you, Peyton. *Conozco tu alma,*" she whispered, her fingertips now trailing across her chest. "This heart? It belongs to me. You're mine, *tentadora.*"

A few tears slipped from Peyton's eyes as she looked at Hadina. "Your lies are as sweet as honey, Hadi, but it only makes it hurt more when you eventually sting me."

"Never again," Hadina said quietly, cupping Peyton's face in her hands. "I swear."

"Please leave," Peyton cried, her tears falling heavier. "Leave before you break my heart all over again."

"No," Hadina answered with resoluteness. "I won't ever leave you again."

Peyton groaned, sniffling as she looked at the ceiling. When she finally returned her gaze to Hadina, there was a sad surrender in her eyes. "God, I hate you. I hate you so much it hurts. But I love you more than I could ever hate you, and somehow that hurts more."

Before Hadina could formulate an answer, Peyton crashed her lips against hers and Hadina let out a sigh. Never before had a kiss ever felt like coming home.

CHAPTER 11

Sunlight trickled in through the gap of the closed curtains, waking Peyton from her sleep. She stretched, groaning as her bruised skin moved and disturbed the wounds across her body. She was about to roll onto her side before she felt an arm tighten around her waist.

Hadina hummed in her sleep, rubbing her face against Peyton's arm with a contented sigh. Peyton stared at her, avoiding the urge to reach out and run her fingertips across Hadina's beautiful features. It had felt like years since she'd been in bed beside the woman she loved, and longer still since she had felt her touch.

When Hadina had come storming back to the room last night, Peyton had been furious. She had told her to leave, but Hadina had chosen to ignore her. But mostly, Peyton was just exhausted. She had been fighting for her life for weeks, and she didn't want to have to fight Hadina too. The moment Hadina had invaded her personal space, Peyton had caved.

Her heart was already Hadina's—what was the worst that could happen?

She had already been through the worst, or as close to it as she was willing to imagine. And if she was being really honest with herself, Hadina fighting for her despite her protests was what she wanted. But being honest with herself wasn't Peyton's strong suit. Living in denial and delusion was way easier.

"*Buenos días, tentadora,*" Hadina said softly, loosening her grip on Peyton.

Peyton looked at her and offered a small smile. "Good morning, Hadi."

Hadina peered around the room, taking in the sunlight. "Did you get any sleep?"

"Some. Sleeping is hard right now," Peyton admitted quietly. "I see things I don't want to see when I close my eyes for more than a minute, not to mention, every spot on my body seems to protest every position."

Lacing their fingers together, Hadina squeezed her hand. "That won't last forever. But I'm sorry you have to go through it at all. Your body will heal in time. Unfortunately, nightmares have a way of plaguing us in the most terrifying ways. If I could take them from you, I would. If I could suffer them instead of you, I would."

"I wouldn't wish it on you."

Hadina shrugged. "I probably deserve it. I definitely deserve it more than you."

The sadness and guilt in Hadina's voice reminded Peyton of why she had fallen in love with the Adis ice queen. While the woman had a hard shell protecting her, she was soft and vulnerable inside—Peyton was the only person ever really allowed to see it.

"I don't think anyone deserves it. Not really. Although," Peyton said with a slight smirk, "I wouldn't mind if Demi faced some nightmares of her own. That woman probably does deserve it."

Hadina sat up at that, her face transforming into a beautiful mask of vengeance. "I'll make sure that she experiences a lifetime worth of nightmares, for you and for everyone else she's ever harmed."

Peyton brought her hand up to Hadina's cheek, looking into her eyes and seeing the fire within them. "Only if I'm by your side while you do. We do it together."

"We do everything together from here on out," Hadina agreed, propping herself up on her elbows.

Leaning forward slowly, Hadina captured Peyton's lips in a gentle kiss. Despite the fact that they had spent hours making out last night until Peyton's lips were swollen and sore, she still craved Hadina's kisses like they were the air she needed to breathe.

Deepening the kiss and throwing her arms around Hadina's shoulders, Peyton groaned. She would never get her fill of this woman and the absolutely tantalizing way she kissed her. When Hadina's tongue teased at her lips, Peyton opened up for her and relished in the taste. She tugged at Hadina to move her hands, get rid of the clothing barrier between them, but Hadina shook her head with a soft chuckle, separating them a little.

"Ay, baby, you're still healing!" she admonished, glancing worriedly at the bruises across Peyton's skin.

Peyton smirked, shrugging. "I'd heal better if we were both naked. Something about body heat?"

Hadina swatted at Peyton's roaming hands. "*¡Necia!* That's for fucking frostbite! As far as I can tell, you're plenty hot right now."

"Spoilsport," Peyton muttered, groaning as she got out of bed. "Guess I'll go take a shower."

"I could join you..."

"You could but since you won't let me see you naked, you're not getting to see *me* naked." Peyton laughed at the curses Hadina muttered to her back as she made her way into the ensuite bathroom. "I would really love a coffee for getting out of the shower, if you're feeling dutiful!"

"Anything you want will be yours," Hadina replied, sending a fresh set of butterflies free in Peyton's gut for the first time since she returned home.

Hadina had told her—in her strictest voice—that she had to rest and relax until her body wasn't in complete agony. While Peyton wanted to rebel against being told what to do, she really was in agony and she knew she needed the rest. So after her shower and coffee, Hadina went off to work while Peyton stayed in bed watching movies. But the thing about getting kidnapped, abused, and almost murdered was that it really put a damper on how entertaining fiction was.

A knock at the door a few hours later interrupted her rather boring movie marathon. "It's Piper."

Peyton sighed. While she loved Piper, she wanted nothing more than to just chill on her own. But Piper had never done her wrong, that much she knew.

"Come in."

Piper opened the door, popping her head inside. "Up for some company?"

Peyton plastered on a fake smile. "Sure! Come on in."

"I just wanted to check in on you," Piper said, spinning her curly hair around until it resembled a bun on top of her head. She clambered up onto the bed beside Peyton, nudging their shoulders. "I'm always here if you need to talk."

"I don't want to talk," Peyton answered bluntly. "I have everything playing on repeat in my mind. Talking won't help that."

Piper pursed her plump lips, nodding ever so slightly. "I can understand that. How about we just be sloths and watch trash TV then? Keep your mind distracted."

Peyton could hardly imagine how Piper of all people would be able to understand, but she appreciated the sentiment. "Sounds good to me."

Handing Piper the control, they flipped through a bunch of channels before Piper landed on some sort of soap opera. She began to explain to Peyton what the show was about, but Peyton couldn't take any of it in. She just nodded and pretended to focus on the show, laughing at whatever quips elicited a giggle from Piper.

"It was...my mom. She's the one who hit me."

Without realizing, the show had delved into a more serious tone. A young boy bore bruises on his arm which caught the attention of his teacher. The pain in his voice was what caught Peyton's attention, but the fact it was his mother hurting him? Something inside her snapped and she began to sob uncontrollably.

"Shit, Pey... I'm so sorry!" Piper turned the TV off and wrapped her arms around Peyton.

The tightness of Piper's grip on her was agony on her damaged body, but Peyton stayed in the embrace. She would rather feel the physical pain of a comforting hug, than the mental anguish over what Demi had done to her.

"I hate this!" Peyton cried out between sobs. "I feel so freaking weak, Piper. I can't believe this is who I am now. I'm a weak, cowardly *murderer*!"

Piper rocked them slightly, running her hand over Peyton's hair. "You're neither weak nor cowardly, Peyton Dimitra. And for the other part—you had no choice. It was self defense."

Peyton shook her head, pulling out of Piper's grip. "No, you don't understand! It wasn't self defense. I killed those men and I felt *joy*. I was happy that I was taking their lives after they made me suffer so much. Do you know how wrong that is? I took two human lives and I can't believe that's who I am now. Even if they did deserve it, it was wrong."

"It's something you have to learn to deal with, Pey. Because you can't let it eat you up like this."

"I'm so scared," she admitted. "I'm scared of how angry I am. It's a fire in me and no matter what I do, it won't extinguish. And I don't think it ever will; at least not until Demi is dead in the ground. And even that is so fucked up." Peyton took a deep breath, her sobs making her body shudder. "I never thought my life would turn out like this, Piper. And I love Hadi, with everything in me, and I don't want to lose her, but I don't know how to do this. I'm going to be a weakness in the Adis chain and I can't do that to you all."

Piper hushed her gently, grabbing her some tissue from the bathroom to wipe her face. "You're not a weakness and you never will be. I always thought of myself like that too. I'm the baby sister, the creative one, the one who stayed as far away from the family business as possible. But neither of my sisters have ever viewed me as weak. If you choose to be part of the family, it doesn't mean you have to be part of the business."

"That's the thing," Peyton mumbled, "I really *want* to be part of the business. And that scares me even more."

"What about therapy?"

Peyton balked. "Are you joking? I can't tell anyone any of this."

"Not that kind of therapy. *Adis therapy.*" Piper crossed her legs, letting her hands fall into her lap. "When my mom died, I was so little, but I've grown up with so many memories of a woman who loved me more than she loved herself. That's an amazing feeling, for sure, but it's also so much pressure. And the loss of that love, combined with knowing I had to make myself worthy of it as I grew, pushed me into being someone you'd never recognize. I was so angry and bitter and I lashed out at everyone.

"I remember running away once. I was barely at the edge of

town when Adrian pulled up beside me in one of the family cars. He told me to get in and when I did, he turned the car off. We sat there for an hour, in silence, until I finally broke down. He told me that my mom would have wanted me to grow up being whoever *I* wanted to be, and that simple piece of information changed my life."

Despite her hurt, Peyton smiled at the tenderness in Piper's voice. The emotion was pouring from her, and Peyton didn't miss the faint blush at the mention of Harris.

"He took me to some of our training locations. Taught me how to box, let me beat the shit out of some punching bags. Took me to a shooting range. Made me go running. He made me try everything to help me release the rage and the hurt that was stuck inside me."

Peyton sighed. "I love that he did that for you; really, I do. But I'm hardly in a fit state for that type of therapy."

Piper patted Peyton's hand. "Adis therapy will be there for you when you're healed and ready, because those feelings don't just go away." She grinned, leaning forward as though they were sharing a secret. "Besides, Adis & Co. have a shrink on the books too, just in case you do want to go the traditional way."

Wiping at her tear stained cheeks, Peyton snorted. "That's good to know."

"Either way, we're all here for you, Pey. You're a strong, beautiful badass and you have an entire family by your side now. You don't have to go it alone."

CHAPTER 12

TIME PASSING FOR SOMEONE TO HEAL WAS THE SLOWEST THE WORLD EVER moved. At least, that's what it felt like to Peyton. She'd been cocooned in the Adis house for over a week, both Hadina and Piper watching over her like she was a broken doll. It pissed her off. She loved them for it, for the kindness they showed her, but she hated sitting fucking still.

What she really wanted was to be outside, breathing in the fresh air and reminding herself that she was free.

She hadn't been quite ready to see or speak to Don yet—after all, even Hadina was still walking on eggshells around her—but she missed when they used to garden together, sitting outside and talking about everything until the sun went down.

"I'll be back late tonight. Do you want me to sleep in my own room so I don't wake you?" Hadina asked, tucking her gun into her waist holder.

Peyton shook her head. "We spent too long apart. But maybe

I'll sleep in your room tonight? I could do with a change of scenery."

Hadina smiled at that, her eyes flashing with hunger as they roved over Peyton's body. "I'll never say no to having you in my bed, in any capacity, *tentadora*." She leaned over, pressing a light kiss to her lips. She was being so cautious with Peyton which was another thing driving her mad...

"Get some rest. I love you," Hadina said into her hair, pressing a kiss to the top of her head.

"I love you, too," Peyton replied, feeling the same familiar tug at her insides. The whole I love you thing was new to them both, but it still made her feel giddy whenever she heard Hadina say the words. It was a declaration between them. "Be safe."

"*Siempre.*"

An hour passed after Hadina left before Peyton felt so overwhelmed with boredom that she had to leave her room. She pulled on her combat boots and tied her hair up in a ponytail, avoiding looking in the mirror as she did so. She knew, if she looked, that she'd see fading bruises and cuts that were almost healed; they should have been a reminder that she was healing, but they'd only remind her of what she'd been through.

Denial was her newest best friend.

She was glad that the house was practically empty as she walked through it. Piper and Harris must have went into the office with Hadina, and Peyton knew Don was probably reading in the study so he didn't cross her path. She'd have to speak to him at some point, but she wasn't quite ready yet.

Peyton breathed a sigh of relief as she stepped into the backyard, the sun beating down on her and sound of birds chirping filling the air. She walked slowly, admiring the flowers that were now blooming and the trees which were bearing fruit.

It had been so long since she'd sat on the patio area; today seemed like it was finally time for her to do it. She was so busy in her own head, thinking of what it was like when she'd first arrived at the Adis house, that Peyton didn't notice someone already sitting there.

"You smoke?" Zellie asked, holding out her packet of cigarettes.

Peyton's blood boiled. "Don't you dare fucking speak to me like you aren't the cause of literally everything bad that's happened to me!"

Zellie rolled her eyes and before Peyton knew what she was doing, she was flying towards Zellie, fist poised to hit.

Zellie stood, sidestepping Peyton's attempted punch with ease. "Oh, please. What the hell was that?"

"I'm going to fucking kill you!" Peyton screamed, lurching forward.

"You'll have to try harder than that if you want to kill me. You can't even hit me."

Zellie stubbed her cigarette out in the ashtray and stepped onto the grass, staring at Peyton expectantly. "Well, if you want to hit me, do it. You're right—the shitty things in your life were primarily caused by me. So, go for it. *¡Pégame!* But I won't make it easy for you."

Peyton glared at the woman, all poised and perfect. She looked like a model, but Peyton knew she was nothing but venom beneath. This was the perfect time to beat the shit out of her in retribution for her sister...for herself.

Stepping closer, Peyton followed Zellie onto the grass, squaring her shoulders. She watched for a moment, before creating a fist and throwing her right arm in a curve. This time, it did make contact—with Zellie's shoulder. The Adis sister laughed coldly, motioning for Peyton to try again.

So she did.

Hit after hit, Peyton circled Zellie and tried to land a punch to the woman she hated. Zellie was right when she said she wasn't going to make it easy for her; she barely managed to make contact.

Kicking her leg out, Peyton was sure she was going to catch Zellie off guard, but she simply hit her leg out of the way, causing Peyton to lose balance and fall on her ass.

"Gotta do better than that, *niñita*."

"My sister is dead because of you," Peyton seethed, pushing herself back onto her feet. "You deserve to be dead, not her!"

"Probably," Zellie agreed, grinning like a madwoman as Peyton finally landed a punch. Her first connected with Zellie's nose, the bone crunching before blood started pouring out. Zellie just continued to grin, even as the blood ran down and into her mouth.

"I hate you!"

"Good. Use your hate. Stop being a fucking pushover and own your shit. You're angry? *¡Haz algo al respecto!*"

Zellie's words unleashed a fire in Peyton's soul and she raged, running forward. She threw her arms ferociously, again and again, until she finally felt her hands meet flesh. She punched and punched, blind anger taking over her, unaware of herself.

"You killed my fucking sister!" Peyton screamed. Just as she was about to hit one last blow, Zellie flipped them over, pinning Peyton's arms against her stomach. Blood dripped down the woman's face, her nose obviously broken, her lips burst, and her eyes already showing signs of bruising.

"Yes, I am the reason your sister is dead. And look, now you've got my blood as revenge. But you will never get free reign to hit me like this again. *¿Tu me entiendes?* If you want to get that anger out, use that hate eating you from the inside out, I can show you how to do it. I can teach you how to fight in ways Hadina can't."

Zellie let go of Peyton's arms, standing up and wiping her mouth with the sleeve of her shirt. She looked down at Peyton and for the first time, Peyton saw something human in her eyes.

"I know it won't mean anything," Zellie said, her voice almost soft, "But I'm sorry your sister was a casualty of the shit I started. I'm sorry that you were a casualty of it, too. My sister loves you and...well, I love my sister, in my own way. So, let me teach you so that you don't die on her, okay? She can't lose you."

Leaving Peyton laying on the grass, breathless and defeated, Zellie walked away.

"What the fuck just happened?" Peyton whispered aloud to herself, before bursting into tears.

CHAPTER 13

Dusk had settled across the sky by the time Hadina pulled her car into the driveway. It had been a long day and exhaustion was picking at her bones. Still, she'd made time on her way home to pick up a couple of greasy burgers and fries for her and Peyton to eat in bed—she needed the comfort of unhealthy food in the safety net of the woman she loved. There was no-one else she would ever let see her pig out on fast food.

She tried to ignore how frustrated she felt as she quietly entered her family home, locking the door and punching in the security code behind her to reset the alarms. To say she was pissed at their inability to find Demi would be an understatement, and Hadina couldn't help but feel like she was letting Peyton down. *Again.* She had promised to find her, to help her love find vengeance for everything that had been done to her, and yet Hadina was returning home empty handed again.

Harris and Piper opted to stay another few hours at the office, saying they'd try to come up with some more people to speak to or hide-outs to check for that *puta*. Hadina knew that they were being honest, in part, but she wasn't oblivious to the connection sparking between them either. Piper had always loved Adrian and while she and Zellie had always viewed him as the annoying, but ever loyal, brother to them, there was another type of devotion that shone in Piper's eyes when she looked at him. But Piper was so very cautious about ever getting close to anyone and Hadina just hoped Adrian wouldn't betray her vulnerability by toying with her emotions—it would really fucking suck if she had to kill him for being a dumbass and thinking with his dick.

Hadina paused outside her bedroom door, taking a deep breath to calm herself. While she was always collected and kept her composure at the best of times, anxiety had begun to creep its way into her heart when Peyton was taken and even though she was home again, Hadina couldn't seem to shake the feeling of dread that would wash over her. She ached to drown it in the bottom of a liquor bottle, but she'd promised to try and do better and she hated breaking promises. Instead, she was downing a cocktail of vitamins every morning to try and rejuvenate her liver to lessen the blow of the damage she'd already done. Besides, there was nobody to look after *her* if she allowed herself to drink away her emotions, no matter how badly she wanted to.

"Is that you, Hadi?" Peyton's groggy voice called to her as she opened the door.

"Yeah, it's me, baby." Hadina kicked the door closed behind her and smiled at the sight of Peyton sprawled out on top of her bed, her entire body on show besides the tiny lace panties covering her pussy. Hadina's mouth watered and she knew it wasn't for the burgers in her hand.

Peyton hummed sleepily, yawning as she stretched and woke herself up. "I'm glad you're home. I missed you."

Kicking off her shoes, Hadina climbed onto the bed beside

Peyton, depositing the bag of food on her bedside table. She leaned down and pressed a soft kiss to her love's lips, relishing in the taste. Peyton let out a soft hiss and Hadina pulled back. "*Tentadora,* what's wrong?"

Flicking the switch to turn her lamp on, Hadina gasped as she looked at Peyton. Where her previous bruises were healing and fading, new ones blossomed across her skin. Her lip was burst in two places, a fresh bead of blood forming at each cut.

"What the fuck happened and why didn't you call me immediately?" Hadina raged, gripping Peyton's chin in her hand so she could maneuver her face and see the full extent of her injuries.

Peyton batted her hand away, shifting so she was sitting up at eye level with Hadina. "You should see the other person." Seeing that Hadina didn't find her little joke funny, Peyton rolled her eyes. "I dealt with some of my shit."

She could barely contain her anger as she stared at Peyton, her hands trembling with an ache to hurt whoever had done this to her. "I'm not laughing. Tell me what happened."

"I–I ran into Zellie. Seeing her just unleashed my anger and I–"

"*Me la voy a chingar!*" Hadina interrupted, ready to go and kill her sister for betraying her again, for hurting the one person she loved.

Peyton grabbed her arm, pulling her back to a seated position, shaking her head. "Calm down, Hadi. I'm okay. This... You can't blame Zellie for what happened."

Hadina scoffed. "Like fucking hell I can't! She put her hands on you, baby. *AGAIN!*"

"I put my hands on her first."

That caused Hadina to still. She tilted her head as she looked at Peyton in confusion. "You *what?* I need you to tell me exactly what happened because right now I'm extremely confused and I'm ready to set my sister on fire if she even looks at you again."

Hadina sat silently as Peyton told her what happened while

she was at work. The second she mentioned Zellie hitting her back, Hadina had to clutch her hands together in her lap to stop herself from throwing something at the wall. She was furious that her sister had hurt her *tentadora* but she was even angrier at herself for not being there with her.

Still, it did give her a little buzz of pride as Peyton detailed just how many blows she'd managed to get in.

"I'm so angry at you," Hadina said softly, without any true depth to her voice. "You should never have hit her—not because you're not capable of fighting, or that she doesn't deserve it, but because she's had *years* of training on you and could easily have hurt you. You're lucky she didn't kill you just for attempting it."

"I'm sorry," Peyton said, clutching Hadina's hands. "I know it was foolish but I saw red. I needed a release and hitting her did the trick. Besides, I found her weakness."

Hadina raised a brow, smirking slightly. "I didn't think my sister cared enough about anything to have a weakness. Do tell."

Peyton returned her smirk and raised brow, amusement glistening in her eyes. "*You.* She loves her family—she loves *you.* She won't hurt me, not intentionally, because it would hurt you."

It took Hadina off guard, whatever words she had on her tongue dying silently. Her relationship with her sister had long been broken, but she had to admit to herself that she did love Zellie, in a fucked up way. But it still came as a surprise to her that her sister would admit returning that sibling love to anyone else, especially Peyton, knowing she would tell Hadina. Maybe that was exactly *why* she had chosen to say it to Peyton.

Hadina's head hurt thinking about it.

"So..." Peyton said, leaning back to rest against her pillows. "What do you think about me getting some training with Zellie?"

Hadina shifted, straddling Peyton's waist with her legs, her hands placed on her hips as she circled Peyton's soft, exposed skin.

"I think I'd murder my own sister if she made you any more bruised and bloodied than you are right now."

Peyton chuckled softly, cupping Hadina's cheek tenderly and running her thumb across her cheekbone. "Surely it's better for me to be bruised and bloody learning how to defend myself more than it is for me to get the shit beaten out of me again and I'm unable to stop it?"

Her heart almost stopped in her chest as Hadina imagined Peyton going through anything more than what she'd already suffered. She knew her *tentadora* was right, even if it hurt her to think about it.

"Are you trying to say my training was subpar?" Hadina questioned, leaning forward to press a kiss against the column of Peyton's throat. She heard the woman's short intake of breath and Hadina smiled smugly to herself at the effect she knew she had on Peyton.

"I would never suggest such a thing," Peyton said quietly, her voice breathy as Hadina's tongue licked over her jaw. "But I do know that you'd go somewhat easier on me because you don't want to see me hurt. Zellie wouldn't care."

"Hm," Hadina hummed, her mouth trailing small kisses and licks all across Peyton's exposed chest. Reaching her collarbone, Hadina kissed softly before biting down on the skin, eliciting a sharp gasp from Peyton. She sat back, a devious smile etched onto her face as she looked at Peyton's hungry eyes. "You're wrong— sometimes I *really* like seeing you a little hurt. But only on my terms."

CHAPTER 14

EVEN THOUGH HER BODY HURT AND SHE WASN'T ANYWHERE NEAR HEALED, Peyton craved Hadina. She wanted to be *hurt* by her, to be bitten and bruised in the most delicious way.

"I think you should show me..." she heard herself say, a sly smirk creeping onto her face.

Hadina's eyes widened and her nostrils flared, her mouth twitching. But a second later, she shook her head and Peyton felt her heart deflate. "You're still hurt. You're *more* hurt now, after your little stunt today. I don't want to cause you any more pain. Fooling around can wait."

"I feel fine," Peyton countered. It had been so long since she had felt Hadina come undone, since they had shared breathless kisses and needy touches.

"I'm scared, Peyton," Hadina admitted, her face screwing up as though it hurt her to say it out loud. "You...you were broken when I got you back. I don't want to be the reason you break again because if I'm the reason, it means I won't be the one to be able to bring you back."

Peyton sighed. This damn woman. So tough and angry, yet sensitive and soft and worry-filled, only for her. She both loved and hated it.

"Your dad once told me that fear is natural. That we have to decide whether or not we'll let it consume us. I won't let fear dictate my life anymore, Hadi, and I won't let you live in fear either." Grabbing her face, Peyton pressed her lips against Hadina's in a rough, passionate kiss. She felt her relax in her touch, her mouth opening up to allow Peyton better access.

When they pulled apart, Hadina rolled her eyes and let out a chuckle. "For the record, I would greatly appreciate it if you refrained from mentioning my dad in your monologue to seduce me in the future."

Peyton snorted, nodding her head. "Duly noted. Now, will you *please* fuck me?"

The playful edge to Hadina's expression turned into something darker and Peyton's core tightened in response. She was so ready to come undone.

Hadina grinned. She reached out, running her hands through Peyton's hair before grabbing a few strands between her fingers, tightening her grip and pulling her head back. "Tell me what you want, *tentadora*. I'll give you anything you ask for."

Peyton could feel her heartbeat speed up in her chest as adrenaline pumped through her veins. She knew Hadina meant it; she would give her whatever she wanted, however she wanted it. Luckily for Peyton, she knew exactly what she was craving.

"I want it rough. I want you to fuck me hard, to leave me with marks and bruises from the woman I love to erase the ones from anyone else who's touched me." She licked her lips, already desperate for Hadina's touch. "I want you to help me release the rage beneath my skin so that I come undone with your name on my lips."

"*Como quieras, mi amor.*"

Hadina crashed her lips against Peyton's, her fingers tightening in Peyton's hair. With her free hand, Hadina got to work and began to tease Peyton's nipples, twisting and flicking the sensitive points with delicate cruelty.

Peyton groaned as Hadina bit down on her lip hard, drawing blood as a metallic tang laced their desperate kisses. She reached out to touch Hadina, her hands fumbling to remove her clothes. Hadina laughed against her before she looked down and ripped her shirt open in one tug, buttons flying across the room.

"So messy," Peyton admonished.

"Just like you're about to be," Hadina retorted.

Peyton grabbed at Hadina's breasts through the lace of her bra, relishing in being able to touch her like this again. She roamed her fingers across Hadina's beautiful skin, all smooth contours and beautiful curves.

She was so enamored that she let out a soft gasp when Hadina's fingers brushed her aching pussy through the thin material of her panties. She knew she wouldn't last long under Hadina's expert touches and perfect teasing. The woman was a master at giving orgasms.

"God, I've missed touching you," Hadina said on a whisper, almost like she hadn't meant to say it aloud.

Climbing off her, Hadina flipped Peyton onto her stomach. Her hand connected with Peyton's ass in a hard slap, causing her to shriek as a wave of pleasure rolled over her. Obviously pleased with her response, Hadina slapped her other ass cheek, hard enough that Peyton could feel the welt of her handprint. Her pussy weeped as she moaned, shoving her ass back in a desperate attempt to make Hadina slap her again. Hadina happily complied.

She could feel herself starting to lose control, all her pent up anger seeping out as Hadina touched her, claimed her. It was what she'd wanted and more—Hadina never failed to deliver.

"More!" Peyton cried out, begging to be used.

Hadina's answering laugh was a dark, twisted thing that sent shivers up Peyton's spine in excitement. She felt a hand wrap around her throat, pulling her up onto her knees. Hadina's fingers tightened around her column and Peyton's breasts heaved heavily. She began to work them herself, twisting and tugging at her nipples and massaging aching skin.

"That's it, baby. Play with those gorgeous tits while I pay some attention to this glorious pussy," Hadina groaned into her ear.

Slipping a finger between her folds, Hadina began to slowly—punishingly so—work her. Instead of trying to tease and stretch her out like she normally did, Hadina thrust two fingers inside her straight away and Peyton cried out in blissful satisfaction. Hadina pressed her thumb against Peyton's clit, working it hard as she thrust her fingers in and out of her pussy in tandem.

Peyton threw her back against Hadina's shoulders as she rolled her hips, creating a delicious friction and riding Hadina's fingers as they pumped into her. Hadina responded by tightening her grip on her throat, pressing just enough to make it harder for Peyton to breathe. The combination had her almost ready to fall off the edge.

"I didn't tell you to stop touching yourself. You wouldn't want me to have to stop since you're being naughty and not listening to my instructions, would you? Do as you're told, *tentadora*."

Peyton bit down on her lip at the menacing edge to Hadina's voice, though she could hear Hadina's own breathlessness. She was getting off on this as much as Peyton.

Doing as she was told—because there was absolutely no fucking way she'd let Hadina stop now—Peyton went back to massaging her tits, digging her fingernails into the soft skin as Hadina added a third finger to her rigorous treatment of her pussy.

"That's my good girl. Look at how well you do what I tell you. Are you ready to come for me?" Hadina asked.

Peyton nodded, her voice catching in the back of her throat.

"Use your words."

"Fuck, God, yes! Hadina, *please*!" Peyton begged, her voice catching as her breathing constricted under Hadina's grip on her throat. "Make me scream!"

Tears slipped down her cheeks as waves of pleasure rolled over her, her whole body trembling and aching for release. Hadina chuckled at her wheezing begs and pressed a kiss to the side of her neck.

"Don't forget—*I'm* the only one who gets to mark this pretty skin," she whispered in her ear before biting down and sucking on Peyton's shoulder.

The combination of pain and pleasure was too much for Peyton to bear and she cracked, diving off the deep end. She screamed out, Hadina's name falling out of her lips like some sort of chant as she soared higher, ecstasy enveloping her entirely.

Hadina loosened her grip on her throat and used that hand to tilt Peyton's face to the side. She captured her lips in a rough, messy kiss as she continued to pump her fingers into Peyton's soaking pussy until she had ridden her orgasm out completely. When she eventually pulled her fingers free, Peyton wanted to weep at the lack of them inside her.

She must have made a noise of protest because Hadina laughed against her lips, before she brought her hand to her mouth and licked Peyton's juices clean off her.

"Don't worry, baby," Hadina said, grinning at her, "That was just round one. You wanted rough and messy and to get your rage out? I'll have you screaming all night until you don't have any voice left."

Peyton shivered and let her body fall back against Hadina.

If that was only round one, she couldn't wait to see what the rest of the night brought her.

Peyton didn't remember falling asleep but it must have been sometime after their third round, well into the night. Hadina had teased and played with her until she was nothing but bones and spent orgasms.

She looked beside her, expecting to see Hadina tucked in at her side, but the bed was empty. The sheets were ruffled and still warm, so she knew that Hadina had to have only *just* left. It tugged deep in her chest, seeing that empty side of the bed.

Throwing the sheets off, Peyton climbed out of bed and pulled on a robe. She made her way towards the bedroom door, hearing Hadina's muffled voice as she spoke on the phone. Peyton cracked the door open and pressed her ear against the small, open space to listen.

"*Cálmate, hermano. Ella está a salvo.* She's okay, I promise. Nobody knows where she is."

A chill went down Peyton's spine as she listened. She didn't know who Hadina was referring to, but it sure as hell wasn't her.

"Ay, I know you're worried, Darío, but watch your fucking tone. I'm telling you—I *know* she's safe. *Me aseguré de ello.* Nobody will hurt her." Hadina sighed, leaning back against the wall with the phone to her ear, eyes closed and rubbing her temples with her free hand. Peyton could hear the indistinct sound of a male voice, tone raised, but she was too far away to make out what he was saying. "I don't know what's happening with you and I don't want to know unless it's necessary, but trust me, she is safe. You know I love her, *hermano. Ella es familia.* Nobody will hurt Itza or they'll be facing your wrath *and* mine. *Sí. Sí. Hablar pronto. Ta bueno.*"

Hadina hung up the phone with her eyes still closed. Peyton

threw open the door and let it slam against the wall, startling the woman before her.

"Who the fuck is Itza and why have you never mentioned her to me?" Peyton yelled, inching back when Hadina moved forward. She held up a hand, halting her. "If you're lying to me or cheating on me, I swear to fucking God, I will murder you *and* your little whore before I leave your life for good. You get one chance to tell me the truth, Hadina. One last fucking chance."

CHAPTER 15

HER HEART BEAT FURIOUSLY IN HER CHEST AS PEYTON STOOD STARING AT her questioningly, anger and accusation in her tone after overhearing Hadina speak to her friend.

"It's not how it sounds."

Peyton rolled her eyes. "How fucking cliche. I thought you were better than that."

"No, really. It's complicated but that was my...acquaintance in Mexico. He was asking for my help."

Hadina stepped forward and tried not to wince in dejection as Peyton stepped back, creating more distance between them.

"You called him *hermano*. I know I don't speak Spanish, Hadi, but I'm not dumb. This Darío dude is hardly an acquaintance if you're calling him brother. I know you don't say shit like that lightly."

She was right, and Hadina had to hide the burst of pride she felt that Peyton had been paying attention. That she was picking up her language, little by little, and understanding the importance of her carefully chosen words. But still, Peyton being right only created more problems for her.

"*Tienes razón.* Darío is a friend, someone I consider family. But he's not someone I ever wanted you to meet, to know, to ever even come into contact with in any way. He is...his organization doesn't honor the same values as Adis & Co."

Peyton threw her hands up angrily. "What the fuck does that even mean, Hadina? Can't you just give a straight answer for once in your life?"

Hadina blew out a breath and leveled her gaze at Peyton. Perhaps her *tentadora* was right; she could handle the truth.

"You want the truth? Fine. You can handle it, but this shit isn't pretty and I was trying to protect you. Darío is part of the cartel world. Well, technically, he is now the Don of his own *familia*. He's not a good person. He's killed way more people than me, and he definitely didn't have a good reason for doing most of it. His cartel deals in drugs, Peyton—and not just weed. He's scary and he's involved in shit that would give you nightmares. He killed his own fucking father."

Peyton gasped, her eyes wide as she stared at Hadina. "What happened to your standards, your code of conduct or whatever you called that bullshit set of rules you clearly don't follow?"

Bristling at her comment, Hadina tilted her head, running a hand along her jaw. "Peyton, I love you and I will let you say anything about me or to me that you want, but the one thing you won't fucking do is insinuate that I don't follow my own code. *¿Entender?* Watch what you fucking say. You don't know the whole story."

"Oh, fuck you, Hadina!" Peyton yelled, spinning on her heels and storming further into the room. "You think you're so big and bad, huh? Well, screw you! I'm not fucking scared of you. You wanted me to be part of this, so tell me the truth or I swear I will walk out that door and not come back."

"*Hijo!* I don't want you to be scared of me. I just want you to give me a chance to explain. My relationship with Darío is complicated."

Peyton spun around and Hadina yelped as she threw the TV controller at her, barely missing her head and smashing against the wall behind her. "Peyton, what the fuck? Calm down!"

"Calm down? Are you for real?" Peyton screamed, launching something else at Hadina. "Why don't you tell me more about your *relationship* with this fucking cartel Don you've never mentioned before?"

Hadina ducked to the side as Peyton continued to throw whatever she could get her hands on. Debris scattered across the floor as many of her bedroom items were thrown and shattered in the process. She held her hands up in surrender, pleading with Peyton. "Ay, Peyton, just let me explain!"

"Fuck your explanations!" Reaching out beside her, Hadina watched as Peyton grabbed for whatever was left on Hadina's drawers to launch.

A rush of panic—mixed with adrenaline, because yes, Hadina Adis really was that fucked up—seized Hadina as she realized the only thing left to grab was one of her daggers. Peyton, in her blind and jealous rage, hadn't realized what she'd picked up. She pulled her arm back, ready to throw, and Hadina did the only thing she could think of; she lurched forward, grabbing Peyton by the shoulders and smacking her hard against the wall, the dagger clattering on the floor between them. Using her body as a prison, Hadina pressed herself against Peyton, sliding her thigh between Peyton's legs to trap her in place.

"*Yo ah pasado por ríos de sangre! He hecho tantas cosas que no podías comprender. ¡No eres una niña estúpida, así que deja de actuar como tal!*" Hadina kept her face pressed close to Peyton's as she ranted in Spanish, her natural impulse taking over. "*¡Déjame explicarte antes de juzgar la situación!*"

Peyton straightened her back and stared at Hadina, her face devoid of emotion. She shoved against Hadina's unmoving frame. "I don't speak Spanish so have some respect and speak to me in a language I'll understand. And for the record, even if I can't understand what you're saying, I still know when you're calling me stupid!"

"*Terca!* I was saying you're *not* stupid!" Hadina said, stepping back to let Peyton move away if she wanted to.

"Well, maybe I'd have known that if you weren't speaking in Spanish!"

"I can't help it! It's natural for me to speak my first language when my girlfriend is acting like a crazy bitch!"

"Crazy, huh?" Peyton countered, stepping back into Hadina's space. "I wasn't crazy before I met you, so what does that say?"

Hadina smiled sardonically and nodded her head once. "It says that you were just waiting for me to unleash that *crazy* hot, insane part of you."

Peyton glared at Hadina, though the tiny beginning of a smirk twitched at her lips. "God, you're frustrating as hell."

"And you really are crazy, but it doesn't mean I don't love it." Hadina laughed and tilted her head as she looked at the woman before her. "Are you sure you're not Latina? Cause damn, you're sure as fuck hot-tempered like us."

Sighing, Peyton ran her hands through her hair and sat on the edge of the sofa, defeated. "I'm not gonna apologize for what just happened because you totally deserved it, but Hadi...I need to know the truth. I love you and I don't want to lose you, but keeping secrets will be the death of us and I can't take that."

Hadina sat beside Peyton and took her hands in her own, bringing them to her lips to kiss softly. "No more secrets. I'll tell you what you want to know, but I need you to promise you won't tell anyone."

Peyton frowned. "You don't trust me?"

"Actually, it's the opposite," Hadina said, smiling softly. "You're the *only* person I trust. Nobody—not even *Papi*—knows about this. It's a secret...*she* is a secret I promised never to share with anyone. It's why I haven't told you before; I wanted to wait until I was sure that you felt the same way about me as I do about you, that you wouldn't run for the hills when you found out."

"I promise, Hadi. Just please, tell me what's going on."

Hadina stood and began to pace her bedroom floor. It helped her think if she kept moving. "One of my first proper cases with the business was to find out more about a trafficking ring happening in Mexico. *Papi* was already buried in so much work and Zellie figured I needed to be thrown in at the deep end, so when the case came up, she made sure it was given straight to me."

"What the fuck? What age were you?"

"Nineteen or twenty, I suppose." Hadina shrugged. "Old enough."

Peyton stared at her, worry etched in her brows as Hadina continued to pace. "So, you went to Mexico?"

Hadina nodded. "Puerto Vallarta, Mexico, to be exact. Beautiful place, but the heart of many warring cartels. One of which ended up being who I was investigating. The Puerto Vallarta cartel. Ruthless and unhinged, they were involved in so much shady shit and it felt like I was being fed to the lions. Every informant I spoke to ended up dead the next day, or seemingly vanished out of thin air."

"Oh, Hadi, that's terrifying. You must have been so scared."

"I was. But the fucked up part of me was excited by the thrill of it, knowing I was in the middle of so much danger. I was young and naive to think that I'd be able to stop the trafficking that was going on. But the one thing that came out of my time there was meeting Darío, the cartel prince."

Hadina stopped pacing and sat beside Peyton again, their thighs pressing together and sending a comforting warmth through her. Peyton placed her hand over Hadina's thigh, tracing light circles along the inside of her pant leg with her thumb.

"Darío was heir to the Puerto Vallarta cartel but his father...there aren't enough words to describe what a vile, evil piece of shit he was. He treated his son like a degenerate and a slave, showing him not a single ounce of love or affection. It's common for cartel Dons to treat their sons like seasoned, glorified assassins, but the way he treated Darío was even worse. It was a new level of cruelty I had never seen before and after meeting Darío, I knew he was nothing like that *puto*.

"I'm almost positive—not that he would ever admit it—that it was Darío who kept me from turning up dead while I was down there. He loathed everything his father stood for, but he was good at playing the game. Darío knew that he had to bide his time if he wanted to eradicate the tainted legacy his father had built."

Peyton paused her gentle petting and tilted her head as she looked at Hadina. "But how does that connect to Itza?"

Hadina's lips tugged into a small smile. "Because Itza is Darío's daughter."

"*What!?*" Peyton gasped.

"She was just a baby when I met Darío and was the sweetest little thing. But Darío's life was so crazy and he knew she was going to be in danger if she stayed in Puerto Vallarta. I recognized his need to be better than his father—for Itza, and for himself—and he saw in return my need to be good, to save the lives of innocent kids. So, he asked me for my help."

Hadina could remember her time in Puerto Vallarta vividly. She had been so young and scared, but she was renewed with purpose that she was learning the skills she needed to one day lead Adis & Co. When Darío had asked her to help him and his daughter, it had struck fear so deep into her heart that she wasn't sure she'd ever get over it. It had been almost fifteen years and yet she still remembered exactly how she felt.

"He knew I had connections through the business, that our number one priority was keeping children safe and hidden from predators. Darío wanted me to take Itza back to Texas with me, hide her so that his father could never find her."

Peyton blew out an unsteady breath. "That must have been so difficult for him. To say goodbye to his daughter. Especially when she was only a baby."

"It was," Hadina agreed. "It killed a part of him. But Itza has always been his priority, his end game. He traveled home with me, made sure that she was safe and that I would be able to protect her. He waited a few weeks, telling his father that he was on business, so that he could check out the safehouse and security I arranged for her. Ever since then, he's been working to dismantle the toxic empire his father built and turn it into something more legitimate."

"But why couldn't you tell Don about it? This had to have been weighing on you all this time."

"Darío didn't know my father or my family. He knew *me*. He needed to trust someone with her and if I told *Papi* or anyone else, I'd have been betraying that trust. I fell in love with that little girl the first time I held her in my arms and I'd do anything to protect her, even if it means keeping her a secret from my own family. She may not be my blood, but I love her just the same. She's my niece and she always will be."

Catching Hadina off guard, Peyton pulled her into a long, slow kiss. It sent delighted shivers down her spine and by the time Peyton extracted herself from Hadina's roaming hands, they were both grinning.

"What was that for?" Hadina asked.

"For showing me again the reason I fell in love with you in the first place. No matter what you do, your heart will always be good, Hadina."

CHAPTER 16

"CAN I MEET HER?"

Peyton felt nervous even asking, knowing how hard Hadina had tried to keep Itza a secret all these years. It still amazed her—and left her a little dumbfounded—that Hadina had practically *raised a child* without any of her family knowing. Though when she evaluated it more closely, Peyton knew that the lives of everyone at Adis & Co. held an air of mystery and secrecy.

Hadina looked at Peyton for a second, her eyes soft as they often were when she looked at her. "I... Yes, I would love that. Why don't you get dressed and I'll make some phone calls to let them know we're coming?"

"Sounds good," Peyton agreed, pressing a soft kiss on Hadi's cheek before disappearing into the bathroom.

She felt renewed after a hot shower and washing her hair, letting the water take away her anxieties with it. Peyton was so used to being on edge that for once, she was happy to just *be* for a moment. By the time she had dried her hair and put on a light layer of makeup, Hadina was already waiting for her in the bedroom, dressed to kill.

"You look so fucking hot when you wear things like that," Peyton said, taking time to let her gaze rove over Hadina's frame. Her woman had decided to wear high waisted black pants, a cropped corset top which was almost see-through, apart from the black ribbing and lace embroidery, and layered it with an oversized blazer. Peyton knew that a pair of polished stilettos would be on Hadina's feet and her mouth watered as she imagined kneeling before Hadina's altered height, messing up those pressed clothes, and devouring her until the shadow queen was nothing but putty in her hands.

"If you keep staring at me like that, I'll tie you to this bed and we won't be going anywhere for a week," Hadina admonished, though Peyton could hear the sultry tone in her voice.

Tilting her head to the side as she licked her lips slowly, Peyton let her eyes wander again. "That sounds like a perfect week to me."

Hadina rolled her eyes and pointed to the closet. "Go choose something to wear. We need to leave soon. I don't want to be too late or it'll disturb Itza's lessons."

Peyton padded over to the racks of clothes, looking for something that said *hi, I'm your aunt's girlfriend and I almost died like three times in the past few weeks, so I really hope you don't hate me because my heart can't take it, kid.* She picked out a vintage-style tweed mini skirt, pairing it with black stockings and a fitted beige sweater. She laced up her combat boots and stood tall, twirling slowly for Hadina to get a good look.

"This okay?"

"*Dios ayúdame.* You look like a school teacher, all sweet and innocent, and it's making me insane that I can't take time to pull your little devil out and make you scream."

Heat pooled between her thighs and Peyton cursed herself for picking a long-sleeved sweater when Hadina had decided to make her feel all hot and bothered. Still, she would never get bored of being the object of Hadina's lust and desire.

"Keep your dirty thoughts in those pants until we get home," Peyton said with a smirk, "and then you can do whatever you want to me."

Hadina grabbed her by the waist, pulling them until they were pressed against each other, and pressed her lips lightly against Peyton's. "Oh, those are dangerous words, *tentadora*. I'm going to hold you to that."

PEYTON PLAYED DJ FOR THE HOUR-LONG DRIVE TO THE RANCH WHERE Hadina housed Itza. She belted out the songs with the confidence of someone with a far better voice than she, but Hadina simply laughed and—much to her surprise—even joined in occasionally.

The second they hit the dirt road down onto the sprawling estate, Peyton let out a gasp. Green fields spread from either side of them, flowers blooming along the edges of the wooden fencing. The closer they got to the house, the fields opened up into large areas obviously used for horse riding, with jumping equipment still set out.

"This place is...beautiful doesn't seem descriptive enough."

Hadina smiled and glanced quickly at Peyton before training her eyes back on the road. "It is. When I first bought it, it was nothing like this. I had intended for it to be a home away from home for me, but Itza needed it more. The whole place has been designed for her, what she likes, her schooling, her hobbies. I wanted it to be the best home it could be for her, especially since Darío couldn't stay with her."

It pained Peyton to know that this little girl had missed

growing up without parents, but she knew Hadina had done every-thing she could to make Itza's life happy and comfortable.

They pulled into the driveway in front of the huge farmhouse. It reminded Peyton of the Adis family home, only more rustic. Flowers were planted in boxes outside of the windows, the walls painted a buttery shade of yellow which cast a beautiful, colorful light on the ranch, and homely touches were added at every glance. Itza was a lucky girl to have grown up with this as her home.

As Peyton got out of the car and stretched her legs, she was surprised by a familiar voice greeting her. "Boss. Peyton. Good to see you both. Everything is all set here; Itza is safe and ready to see you."

"Adrian?! What the fuck are you doing here?" Peyton blurted out before she could stop herself. She spun around to Hadina. "I thought you said nobody knew about Itza."

Hadina shrugged, smirking slightly. "Harris has a unique set of skills I needed. Besides, this fool knows he can't ever betray me—he's seen what I do to people who have."

Adrian blew Hadina a kiss while rolling his eyes. "Love you too, Hadi. But we both know I'd be able to take you in a fight."

"*Pendejo,* keep dreaming. I'd have you gutted before you could open your mouth to say anything."

"Oh yeah? How are you gonna gut me with those shaky ass hands?" he rebutted, his eyes widening immediately as he realized he'd said too much.

Peyton frowned. "What was that about shaky hands?"

Harris scratched the back of his head nervously. "I'm gonna... go check the perimeter again."

"*Pinche puto,*" Hadina muttered as he walked past her, her glare burning into his back. She opened her mouth to explain to Peyton, but was interrupted by an excited screech.

"Tía Hadi!" A young girl came barreling out of the house and launched herself into Hadina's arms, her auburn curls bouncing behind her. She held Hadina in a vice-like grip, one which was returned with even more affection.

Itza pulled back after a long moment, her beautiful face beaming at her aunt. Hadina grinned, cupping the teenager's cheek in her hand. "*Hola, mi belleza. ¿Cómo estás?*"

"*¡Bien! Mejor verte, Tía Hadi.*" Itza's eyes shone brightly as she smiled. Peyton shifted awkwardly on her spot, catching the girl's gaze. "*¿Quién es ella?*"

Hadina grabbed Peyton's hand and squeezed gently, pulling her closer to her. She looked between them, her smile so pure that it made Peyton want to weep. "Itza, this is my partner, Peyton. Peyton, this little firecracker is my niece, Itza."

Itza considered them both for a moment, her eyes evaluating in the exact same way she'd seen Hadina do so many times, before she beamed again. "*Tía* Hadi! You finally let yourself get close to someone? *OH MY GOSH*, wait till I tell my dad!"

Peyton watched as Hadina winced, her face scrunching up. "*Señor ten piedad.* Your father doesn't need to know everything, Itza."

Giggling, Itza shrugged. "He doesn't *need* to know, but he'll absolutely *want* to know! This is so exciting, *Tía*! And PEYTON," she yelled, startling Peyton, "I can't wait to get to know you! You're *so freaking PRETTY!*"

"Oh, thank you!" Peyton said shyly. At the same time, Hadina said, "Itza, leave the woman alone. Calm down."

Itza put a hand on her hip, giving Hadi a look filled with attitude and teenage sass; Peyton had to swallow down her laughter. This girl was full of life and happiness and it warmed Peyton to know that Hadina had her in her life, that she'd been the one to keep this kid safe and help her have an amazing life so far.

And now she got to share in that happiness too.

"Ignore your *tía,* Itza. You can ask me any questions you want because I can't wait to get to know you too. Why don't you show me around inside and then we can–"

"*Sí,* I have some questions, too." Peyton jumped at the voice behind her and spun around to see a man standing in the doorway, fury etched into his features. "Let's start with why there is some random *güera* meeting my daughter without my permission?"

Peyton sensed Hadina's presence as she stepped up behind her, snaking an arm around her waist. The man—who Peyton presumed to be Darío—noted the action, the storm behind his eyes settling in a silent understanding. He didn't change his face, but he offered a very slight nod to Hadina, who returned the gesture.

While Darío had been sizing Peyton up, ready to put a bullet in her, she was sure, Itza had heard his voice and taken off running excitedly.

"Daddy!"

Darío's expression softened and the Puerto Vallarta Don practically beamed as his daughter threw herself into his arms. Peyton knew just from looking at him that the man was built solidly and would not be easily moved, yet he made a show of falling backwards into the doorframe, Itza clinging to him.

"*Te he extrañado, mija.*"

"*Te he extrañado más, papi.*"

As Hadina's fingers massaged gently into her stomach, Peyton realized she didn't have to understand the Spanish being spoken to know that father and daughter had missed each other more than any words could accurately express.

CHAPTER 17

"BRINGING SOMEONE TO MEET MY DAUGHTER WITHOUT TELLING ME FIRST was a risky move, Hadi."

Hadina rolled her eyes. Why did men always think they knew better and could intimidate a woman? The last time she had quivered in fear and thought *I should ask for permission* was... Well, she wasn't sure that had ever happened.

"*No te respondo, pendejo.* I don't have to run shit past you."

Darío's piercing eyes flashed with unchecked rage. "You do when it's about my daughter!"

She got up from where she sat on the sofa, standing to her full height and straightening her back, showing just how little she cared about his pissy anger issues. "*Recuerda con quién estás hablando, hermano.* You only get so many passes because of fear or stress before I will *put you* in your place. *¿Entiéndeme?*"

The cartel Don registered her words and though Hadina could tell that the itch to continue fighting was still brewing beneath his skin—an itch she currently shared—he forced himself to breathe and take a seat in one of the plush armchairs facing the sofa.

It hadn't been long since Hadina had last seen Darío and yet, so much about him had changed. His handsome face, all sharp angles and lines, was as untouched by time as it ever was. His full lips were still pulled into a straight line as he stared hard at his hands. But there was something different about him and Hadina knew in an instant that it was the same changes she had forced herself to go through.

"What's their name?"

Darío looked up at her in confusion. "*¿Qué? ¿Cuyo nombre?*"

"I want to know the name of the person who has you all twisted up inside. You're agitated and I know it's the face of worry when you've left someone you love behind."

"You meddle too much for your boss bitch image, you know that?"

She dropped back down to her seat on the sofa, barking out a laugh as a small smirk twitched at Darío's lips. "Perhaps. Now stop avoiding the question."

"Vicente Vargas."

"Vargas? As in–"

"One and the same."

Hadina barked out another laugh. "Oh, you're fucked. Not only did you let yourself fall in love, you did it with a fucking Vargas? Literally a descendant of one of the most notorious cartels and he falls in *your* lap?"

"Well, actually," Darío said with a shit-eating grin on his face, "he hasn't done that part yet."

"*Hijo!* I don't need the details, you horny little shit."

Darío threw the middle finger at her, his shoulders trembling in silent laughter. "*No finjas que no te estás tirando a esa linda chica blanca.* I'm only *cachondo* because I'm not getting any."

"Ay, watch your mouth when you speak about my woman."

"Your woman, huh?"

"*Sí, soy de ella.*" Hadina grinned as Peyton's fingers curled over her shoulder, squeezing down territorially. She reached up, placing her hand gently over Peyton's. "I don't speak Spanish, but I know when someone is calling me a white girl in any language. It's a pleasure to meet you, Darío, but if you try to assume I'm some basic hoe again, I'll have my knife at your throat and not even my beloved here will be able to stop me."

Darío sucked air through his teeth before a grin matching Hadina's spread across his face. "Damn, Adis, you got yourself a feisty one, huh?"

Posturing, she straightened her back and pulled Peyton down for a long, slow kiss. Once she was done, her woman walked around the sofa and took her seat beside Hadina, crossing her long legs. Hadina entwined their fingers before she turned her attention back to Darío. "Yes, I did. Now, *hermano*, why don't you tell me what you're doing here?"

Darío visited Texas unannounced only when there was something wrong. Normally, he told Hadina ahead of time and it meant that she had time to prepare. Him turning up was great in theory because it meant seeing Itza happy, but it also alerted Hadina to some danger she was unaware of. Something had unsettled the Puerto Vallarta Don and from the look in his eyes, she was about to gear up for war.

"I got a note, like I told you on the phone. Threatening Itza."

Hot, burning fury shot through Hadina's veins like a wildfire. "What do you need? My team will be ready the second you need them."

Darío held up his hand, shaking his head slightly. "I don't need anything yet. You know you are the only person I trust to keep Itza safe, but I had to come and see her for myself. Calling ahead of time was not safe to do." He took a deep breath, blowing it out shakily. Reaching into his breast pocket, he pulled out a cigar, clipped it, and lit it up. "The note said she wouldn't make it to her *quinciñera*. That's only a few months away, Hadina."

"Do you know who is behind the threat?" Peyton asked.

"Maybe. We have some avenues I'm looking into but I have to be careful before taking action. I won't risk my daughter's life."

Peyton nodded, a sadness hanging in the air around her, and Hadina squeezed her hand. She knew that Peyton was wondering what had went wrong in Demi's fucked up brain to make her burn out the maternal instinct that society projected onto women. She didn't blame the woman for not wanting kids, but Hadina blamed her—and wanted to kill her—for the absolute hell she had caused Peyton.

The sound of Itza's laugh echoed throughout the large house, breaking the tension in the room. Darío leaned his head back, taking another puff of his cigar, a small smile on his handsome face.

"She's happy here, huh?"

The question was a loaded one that made Hadina's heart break a little. Darío wanted his daughter to be happy, but it was bittersweet for him to know that she was happy in a home so far away from him. He loved and missed his daughter, Hadina knew, and it broke him to not see her very often.

"She is..." Hadina answered, treading carefully. "She loves the home I've created for her here. But–It's not really *home* when her father isn't here. She may not know you properly, but she *loves* you."

"I want to bring her home."

Hadina began to laugh but stopped abruptly when Peyton tensed beside her. Darío's face stayed stoic and dread hit her gut like a gunshot. "You're not joking."

Darío shrugged. "Like you said, this isn't home. She belongs with me and I belong in Puerto Vallarta. I want her to come home with me; to be with me and *my* family."

"You would be taking her from all she knows," Peyton said softly, squeezing Hadina's hand as though she knew that the fire within her was about to burn out of control. "That doesn't seem fair."

"*Fair?* I have had to live without MY daughter for years. How is *that* fair?!"

Unwavering and without flinching at the anger in his voice, Peyton stood up, facing Darío at her full height. "You have lived without your daughter because of *your* actions. Hadina has been the one to raise your child, keep her safe, show her what unconditional love is. Hadina gave your child a family and now you want to rip her away from that."

"She's right, *hermano,*" Hadina agreed, standing beside her woman. "I understand how you feel—really, I do. But ripping her away from her life here isn't the right thing to do."

Darío puffed from his cigar, his fist clenching and unclenching by his side. He stood and began pacing, his body stiff and tense. "Who are you to tell me what the right thing is? Itza is *mine* and I will make the decisions for her and her future."

Shaking her head, Hadina took a step forward, moving herself into Darío's space. "Firstly, I'll remind you who you are talking to. Here, you are in *my* country and *my* home. The home *I made* for your daughter. The daughter *I* raised. I swore to protect her for you, to love her when you weren't here to do it, and I've done everything you have asked of me." The slight crack in her voice betrayed the emotion Hadina was usually so good at burying beneath the surface. "But Darío, I love that child. She may not be mine—not by blood—but I love her as though she was. And if I truly thought you taking her to Mexico was the best thing for her, I wouldn't stand in your way. Believe me when I say, this is the wrong decision. You can't take her from here and force her into a new, dangerous life overnight."

"*Chinga tu madre!* You don't get to tell me what I can and cannot do. My child belongs with me!"

Hadina threw her hands into the air. "How about you ask Itza what *she* wants?"

"How about you–"

"Enough!" Peyton yelled, positioning herself between Darío and Hadina. "Stop squabbling like fucking children! There are *way* more important things happening right now that require imme-diate attention. This can be discussed later."

Darío sighed, stepping back. "*Sí, ella tiene razón.* We have busi-ness to attend to; enemies to kill. But Hadina," he warned, "You have to get used to the idea of my daughter being with me full time. I'm hosting the annual horse races back home in about three months, and Itza will be one of my riders. She'll be in Mexico with her family and I have no intention of her leaving us again. Three months, *hermana*, and then I want my daughter with me."

CHAPTER 18

AFTER HADINA AND DARÍO'S ARGUMENT, THE HOUSE WAS TENSE. PEYTON assumed the two must have had talks later, because the following days were spent living almost carefree. Peyton got to know both Itza and Darío, and understood why Hadina found herself so attached to both people. But the idea of Itza leaving sparked fear even in her heart, so it was unimaginable how Hadina was feeling.

"Why are we going to this dinner?" she asked Hadina, throwing herself onto the bed as she watched her love shimmy into her dress.

"Because these people are important to Darío, and that little fucker matters to me. I want to meet his family and..."

"You want to see the people Itza will be living with when he takes her from you," Peyton finished for her. Hadina nodded.

"I trust him, but I want to see for myself. Besides, Itza has Darío wrapped around her fingers so someone needs to be there to keep that girl in line."

Peyton chuckled. "Don't pretend she doesn't have you wrapped around her finger too."

Hadina paused from putting on her lipstick, turning her gaze directly to Peyton. Her eyes danced with mischief and Peyton squealed as Hadina leapt onto the bed, straddling her legs. "You're going to ruin my reputation if you say stuff like that."

The black dress had rolled up Hadina's thighs as she climbed onto the bed and Peyton couldn't help but let her hands roam over the exposed skin. She never grew tired of watching as Hadina's eyes closed at her touch, her plump lips parting slightly to breathe heavier. Only Peyton could have that effect on her, and she was absolutely drunk on that knowledge.

"Your reputation," Peyton whispered as she guided her fingertips higher, "Was already ruined the second you decided to fall in love with me. Sorry, not sorry."

Hadina opened her eyes, those dark irises gazing down at Peyton with a devotion so deep that it almost brought tears to her own eyes. "I'm not sorry about it. Falling in love with you was the best thing to ever happen to me, and to the rest of my family. You make us better, *tentadora*."

Peyton allowed herself a second to linger in that look, and that confession, before she sniffed and shook her head. "Okay, enough of this cuteness. We've got to get ready."

"Some of us are already dressed," Hadina commented with a smirk.

"Well, some of us actually have to put work into our appearances, miss *I-roll-out-of-bed-and-look-this-good*."

"Baby, you're the only person in the world who never needs *any* work to look as absolutely breathtaking as you always do. And if anyone tells you otherwise, let me know so that I can rip their limbs from them."

"I'll keep that in mind," Peyton said, chuckling lightly. Her smile dropped almost instantly when a thought popped into her head. "I mean, we both do know one person who could do without a few limbs."

Hadina put her arms around Peyton's waist, bringing her close. "Trust me, baby, her days on this earth are numbered. And when her time comes, she'll be losing more than a few limbs."

THEY ARRIVED AT A BEAUTIFUL ROOFTOP RESTAURANT CALLED *ROSARIO'S* and Hadina immediately had Peyton hand in a vice-like grip. It was a small act of protection and possessiveness, but it still sent delighted shivers down Peyton's back.

"Do you think they'll like me?" Itza asked from Peyton's other side. She reached down and grabbed the young girl's hand, bringing it to her lips in a soft kiss of endearment. "There isn't anyone in the world who could dislike you, Itza."

Itza beamed, clinging tightly to Peyton's side. Peyton could almost imagine her as a small child, running around her legs and looking up at her with those big doe eyes. She had never exactly craved having kids or being a mom—the world was a fucked up place and she hated the idea of bringing a child into that—but Itza had wormed her way into Peyton's heart in an indescribable way and she hated the idea that they would have to say goodbye.

"I'm glad my *tía* has you, Peyton. *Aunt* Peyton."

"And I'm glad she has *you*, little one. That now we both do."

The second the elevator door opened, Itza spotted Darío at the table and took off running. "*Papá!*"

Darío grunted as Itza collided with him, chuckling as she threw her arms around him in a tight hug. Standing together, it was a beautiful thing to see father and daughter embrace each other. Peyton glanced at Hadina and saw that she was feeling the same, though a hint of sadness was etched into the woman's smile and Peyton knew she was thinking how impossible it would be to deny Darío taking his daughter for them to be together.

Peyton hated that Hadina would have to make yet another sacrifice, hurting her own heart more just to please other people. One day...One day, Hadina would stop having to give up pieces of herself for others.

As they walked to the table, Peyton felt Hadina's grip on her hand tighten. Standing beside Darío was Vicente, whom Hadina had described as *kind, respectful, and absolutely deadly*. On his other side was Kat, who Peyton had taken an immediate liking to, also. Both Vicente and Kat were strong, determined people and Peyton could feel the energy pulsing off them in waves. She knew that there was something happening between the three of them, but she wasn't going to pry. Still, she hoped it worked out for them all.

Standing between two handsome, muscled men, was a young woman with long, dark hair cascading down her back. When she turned her gaze to them, Peyton almost gasped. The resemblance to Vicente was uncanny, their honey brown eyes and angled noses exactly the same. Her men—really, there was no other way to describe them after seeing the possessive stance they'd immediately taken up beside her, not unlike the way Hadina was standing at her side—assessed them both, ocean blue and emerald green eyes staring them down. The woman stepped forward, but one of the men pulled her back, forcing her to stand behind them slightly.

Dismissing their show of strength, which seemed futile when they were only there at Hadina's behest, Peyton forced her gaze away. She let her eyes wander around the rooftop terrace, taking note of the closest exits, how many knives were on their table, and just where the visitors' clothes didn't sit quite right, meaning they were concealing their weapons beneath.

"Hadi, I'd like for you to meet the rest of my familia," Darío said as they took their place at the table. "Little Curse is Vicenta, Vin's twin sister and these are her men, Romero and Alvaro."

Hadina raised her brow slightly at Darío's words, her gaze sliding over Romero and Alvaro as their dynamic clicked into place.

Alvaro, the taller of the two men, held Vicenta's hand. His shaven head was almost as striking as his blue eyes, icy and vibrant like the ocean. Romero was the dark to his light, with a head of almost curled black hair, dark brows, and mossy green eyes. He slipped his arm around Vicenta's waist as Peyton smiled, both men sharing a look with each other.

"*Mucho gusto*, Vicenta. *Esta es mi novia*, Peyton." Hadina held out her hand to the woman, a peace offering to dispel the imposing atmosphere around the table.

"*Mucho gusto,* Hadina." Vicenta shook her hand kindly, then turned to do the same to Peyton. "Pleased to meet you, Peyton."

Once introductions were finally complete and everyone chilled out with their *I'm so powerful* looks, wine was served and conversation began to flow. Peyton noted that Vicenta and her men chose to stay relatively silent unless spoken to directly, their watchful gazes always on high alert every time someone moved an inch.

Itza seemed to be enjoying the time with her father, getting to know his friends. Vicente already had a way with the kid, both of them sharing secret smiles and laughing at whispered jokes.

When the dinner plates were almost cleared and everyone was relaxed and full bellied, Peyton leaned forward to speak to Itza. "Did you tell your *papí* what you want for your quinceañera?"

Darío's brows furrowed before he leaned forward. "*¿Qué pasa, hija?* Tell me what you want and I'll get it for you."

She looked up at him with a face that could get away with murder. "You promise?"

"*Calro, mijita,*" he promised, making Hadina sigh in her seat.

"*No manches.*" Peyton smirked at Hadina's frustration. The kid knew how to play them both.

Itza gave her a look that Hadi threw right back at her. When she turned back to her father, Itza's words came out in a rush. "I want two things: the first is to spend next summer vacation in Puerto Vallarta with you. And I also want a purebred Arabian horse —white, if possible."

"Tell you what," Darío finally said after a long few seconds, "I'll get you the horse, and I'll do everything in my power to have our home ready for you. Hopefully by then, you'll be coming home for good."

Itza's eyes lit up but quickly dimmed as she looked over at Hadi and Peyton. "But *tia* Hadi and aunt Peyton—"

"Can come and visit you anytime they want, for however long they want. You can even come here and visit them when you miss them. But this only works if you keep your grades up this year and I get the house ready in time. Deal?"

"Thank you, daddy!" Itza hugged Darío, wrapping her arms around his neck and kissing his cheek.

Peyton could feel Hadina's tension from beside her. So much for giving them three months to get used to the idea. Darío had practically swept Itza out from under Hadina's feet, and there was nothing either of them could say to make it better.

Talk quickly shifted onto other topics, with Itza talking about her schoolwork and riding the horses Hadina had bought for her to practice with.

Alvaro—who seemed to be the peacekeeper of his little trio— caught Itza's attention, leaning forward to speak to her. "You like riding horses, huh? Do you ever ride competitively?"

Peyton bit back her grin and Hadina swore under her breath, rubbing her temples.

"I'm a barrel racer but *tia* Hadi won't let me join any leagues. She says I still need training even though I've beaten everyone's times on the ranch—even Beto."

"Being good and fast is not the problem, Itza," Hadina said, exasperated.

"Then why do I need more training?" Itza pouted.

"Because you don't follow the rules, *niña*. When you cut corners on the rules and try to skip certain lessons just because you think you know better than the trainer, you'll lose, even when you win."

The fourteen year old rolled her eyes, pushing her leftover food around her plate as she replied under her breath, "I actually do know the lessons—it's called reading ahead. You and *papá* taught me that."

Vicente choked on his laughter, using the top of his fingers to lightly pinch Itza's arm. "Sounds just like something he'd teach you, but sometimes going fast isn't always good. Slowing down and taking the advice of those who have been in the game longer than you is beneficial."

"Honestly, that's advice you and your sister need," Kat laughed.

"Hey!" Vicenta and Vicente said in unison.

Peyton giggled. "By the looks of it, everyone at this table needs that advice."

Vicenta huffed, her brows furrowing. "What do you mean, *Blancita?*"

Peyton grinned at the nickname, knowing it was said as an endearment rather than an insult. "Really?" she replied, her eyes looking pointedly at how both Alvaro and Romero held Vicenta's thighs, and Vicente had his arms draped over the back of Itza's chair and Kat beside him, glancing possessively at Darío every few seconds.

Vicenta burst out laughing. "Yeah, me and my brother have the thrill gene. It can't be helped."

"You and that mouth of yours," Hadi said gruffly into Peyton's ear, making her blush hard while biting her lip. She lowered her voice to a whisper, her lips brushing Peyton's soft skin. "I can't wait to put it to good use later."

Peyton felt her blush spread throughout her body, making her cross her legs beneath the table.

"Promise?" she asked with a sly smirk. Hadina's hand slid up her thigh, squeezing gently. It was a silent answer, but Peyton was an expert in Hadina's silence.

"So," Vicenta asked, her honey-coloured eyes shining, "Tell me something I don't know about San Antonio. We're not here long enough to do the whole tourist thing."

She pouted and both of her men rolled their eyes. Alvaro pressed a placating kiss to her temple, while Romero gently squeezed her thigh. "We'll come back for a visit if you wish, *Bruja*."

Itza tilted her head. "Aren't you from here, Vicenta?"

The woman shook her head. A quick darkness passed over her eyes, almost too quick for anyone to notice, but Peyton had perfected that passing look. "Not here. I grew up in Dallas, though Acapulco is definitely home now. I don't know much about San Antonio."

Peyton understood finding a new home for yourself. She'd grown up in a country town, Willowbrooks, and it had been oppressive to say the least. The town itself was beautiful, but when dark moments happened in life, they tended to bleed all over the light. What was once home became a trap, and escaping was the only way to let yourself live again. She'd been lucky to go off to college, and then find her way to San Antonio with the Adis family.

That was the thing too; home wasn't always a place, but a person. Hadina had become Peyton's whole life and she knew that nowhere would ever feel welcome unless Hadina was by her side.

"Did you know the devil once visited San Antonio in the flesh?" Hadina asked. She wore a smirk like a mask, theatrics laced in her voice.

A shiver went down Vicenta's spine. "Tell us the entire story."

"Why don't we go and get some fresh air?" Darío suggest to Itza. The girl shook her head, giggling excitedly. "Absolutely not! I want to hear every word of this story."

"You're too much like your Tía Hadi," Darío muttered.

Hadina leaned back in her chair, waiting a beat to make sure she had everyone's attention.

"The story starts in the seventies with a young girl, just turned sixteen, who decided to disobey her parents for the first time. She led them to believe she was going to the cinema with friends, but instead she went to *El Camaroncito*, a nightclub club in town. As they arrived, they noted a handsome gentleman already making his way around the dance floor. Dressed in a white suit, he caught the eye of everyone in the bar.

"But none caught his eye the way in which our young señorita did. With her young looks, white dress, and the scent of deception covering her skin, she was exactly what he was looking for. The man and young woman danced and danced, allowing him to lure her more. As the night wore on, the girl leaned in for a kiss from her handsome stranger. However, just before their lips touched, a foul scent arose. Burning her nostrils, the girl stepped back, wondering where such a strong smell was coming from."

Itza gasped. "Was it him? The devil?"

Hadina smirked at her niece, lowering her voice to add extra drama. From where Peyton sat beside her woman, she couldn't help but admire her beauty. Hadina was her own personal devil, and Peyton would let herself be lured for the rest of her life.

"The girl happened to look down and in place of the man's dress shoes were now hooves!"

Peyton couldn't help but giggle as Itza and Vicenta squealed at the same time.

"At seeing such a hideous sight, the young woman screamed and broke free from his grip. Her cries for help garnered the attention of all the other club patrons, all of whom saw the hooves. Frantic, *el diablo* ran towards the men's restroom where he ultimately disappeared. Witnesses who had followed him into the restroom say all he left behind was a puff of smoke and the vile stench of sulfur."

The table was silent for a few moments as everyone took in the dark meaning behind the story. Even Itza, that little rebel, sat with her mouth agape.

"Did that really happen?" she asked.

Hadina shrugged. "It's up to you if you believe it. But I will say, my *Mami* told me the story when she was younger and the haunted look on her face... I'm inclined to say it's true."

"And that," Peyton chimed in, despite the cold feeling trickling down her spine, "Is why you shouldn't lie to your parents. Isn't that right, Itza?"

The entire group burst into laughter as Itza stuck her tongue out at Peyton, though there was an edge to everyone's smiles as the night continued.

If anyone should be worried about the devil coming to visit, it was every one of them sitting at that table.

CHAPTER 19

Meeting Darío's family—and by extension, Itza's—went better than Hadina could have expected, yet she felt a heaviness in her heart. Despite their agreement, Darío had encouraged Itza and promised her a future. That was something neither of them could do, and Hadina would be the one to pick up the pieces if the worst were to happen.

It felt like Darío was stealing *her* daughter, and she hated that about herself. But no matter how much she reminded herself that Itza was *just her niece*, Hadina knew that love didn't differentiate like that. She loved Itza fiercely and it didn't matter that they weren't blood related—a piece of her would always belong to that girl.

"Enough moping, Hadina. You have work to do," she muttered to herself.

"You know that talking to yourself is the first sign of delusion, *mija?*"

Hadina looked up, smiling as her father walked into the office, two mugs of coffee in each hand. He handed the larger to her, as he always did, knowing that her body survived on caffeine. "*Hola, Papi.*"

She watched as he slowly lowered himself onto the seat on the opposite side of her desk. He was becoming frailer and it hurt her heart to see it. His gray hair seemed to be whiter, his wrinkles deepening across his face. If she blinked, she could still see the handsome young man he was when she was young, throwing her around the garden and teaching her how to be respectable.

Sometimes, on her rare sentimental days, she missed those years. She'd caught herself wishing for a repeat more than once, just so she could spend her childhood years with both her parents and really treasure every moment with them.

"*¿Qué pasa, Papi? ¿Estás bien?*"

Her father smiled, nodding his head slightly. "*Sí, mija.* I'm perfectly fine. I'm just worried about you. About *all* of my girls."

Hadina *tsk*'d and waved her hand dismissively. "Ay, *Papi*, you worry too much. We're fine. *I am fine.*"

"Then why does my house feel so tense? Something is wrong here, Hadina. Tell me."

"You're a meddlesome old man, you know that?" She let out a long sigh. "I have some... *personal* things I'm trying to battle in my head. And while that's happening, we're all also on high alert for that *pinche perra* who seems to have fallen off the face of the earth."

A worry crease formed between his brows. "Really? Nobody has seen her?"

"Not that we can find. Every lead we get turns out to be a dead end. I just wanna find her and make her pay for what she did to Peyton, *Papi.* She deserves retribution."

Her father studied her for a moment before he hummed. "Well, *mija*, you just need to get your shit together and stop all this *woe is me* attitude."

Hadina sat up straight in her chair, tilting her head slightly as she looked at her father. He was always blunt, straight to the point, but it was rare that he spoke to any of his daughters in such a way. A slow smirk teased at her lips.

"Rude... But I think you're right."

"Of course I'm right," he said, rolling his eyes. "I taught *all of you* what you know. But I also know just what you're capable of. Stop letting Demi Treyva have the upperhand. You're the head of Adis & Co. for a reason, Hadina. Use all of your resources and get that bitch and make her pay."

Her father pushed himself out of the chair and left her alone to think. She gulped down the remainder of her coffee, tapping her fingers against the edge of her desk until an idea sparked in her mind. Hadina had more resources than even her father knew, and she was about to call in *all* the favors she was owed.

<hr>

Two hours later, the entire family was gathered at the Adis & Co. headquarters. Every seat in the conference room was filled, with more bodies crowded around the walls. Sitting to her right was Peyton, staring at her with murder in her eyes and making her feel weak at the knees. To her right, Adrian sat poker-straight, his eyes analyzing and warning the rest of the team to keep their mouths shut until they were asked to speak.

"What's the plan, *hermana?*" Zellie asked, her fingers laced on the table in front of her. She was all business today, which meant she was ready for war.

Hadina clicked a button on the remote in her hand, bringing up a slide of photos on the projector screen behind her. "These are the known associates of Demi Treyva." *Click.* "These are the ones we've already taken out." *Click. Click.* "These *putos* are our next targets. I want them all *taken care of.* These people are all scum. They have beaten and abused women and children, trafficked them, murdered plenty. They do not deserve to live."

"Are they examples? Or should they disappear?" Piper asked. Hadina hated that she was part of this, that she was going to get her hands dirty for the first time, but Piper was close to Peyton. Family and loyalty meant everything to her.

Harris smirked and looked across the table at Piper. "Look who finally joined the party. They should disappear. They don't deserve the luxury of being made examples of."

Piper beamed under his praise and Hadina had to ignore the way Peyton was making faces at her, excited to have noted it too.

Click. "These two men are our key to getting Demi."

"Who are they?" Peyton asked.

Harris fielded the question. "The one on the left is Eddie Poplar. A random foot soldier, but one we'll be able to use to our advantage. The man on the right is Derick Hernandez, a high ranking member of Treyva's organization. We know Demi doesn't care for anyone, but she does value her loyal people. Hernandez happens to be someone extremely loyal to her."

Hadina watched as her *Papi* leaned forward in his chair, his eyes sparkling with the excitement of the hunt. This was where he thrived and while he wouldn't be going out and doing any of the manual labor, Hadina knew he was just grateful to be part of the process. "How do these men lead us to Demi?"

"Because," Hadina replied, her voice stern and filled with the threat of what she was about to say, "We're going to play them against each other. Hernandez won't talk...but he doesn't have to. We're going to torture him and then invite Eddie Poplar to watch as we kill him."

"Mr Poplar will shit his pants," Adrian continued. "He'll see us killing a *high ranking* member of the crew and realize that we would do that so easily to him. He'll sing like a canary and tell us whatever we want to know."

Brushing a strand of dark hair behind her ear, Hadina nodded, tapping her finger on the table. "That's our key. Because once that happens, we're going to exploit the shit out of Poplar. He's going to be given a car—"

"One that obviously has a tracker in it," Harris interjected.

"—and the dead body of Hernandez. He'll be tasked with delivering our little message directly to Demi, all the while exposing her location to us."

The room was quiet for a moment as everyone considered the plan in their heads.

"What if Poplar doesn't know where Treyva is? He's a foot soldier, like you said, so I doubt he's privy to that kind of information."

"You're correct," Hadina agreed. "He won't have access to that information. But when Demi realizes that her entire team has been wiped out, she'll be quick to make herself readily available for anyone who has any information on it. She'll have eyes watching and waiting, and she'll sure as hell want to meet Poplar."

With a nod of her head, Hadina watched as Adrian spread out a state-wide map across the conference table. They had taken time earlier in the day to circle all known whereabouts of Demi's associates, as well as the surrounding areas they'd need to cover. Definite locations were marked with a large X in red, while everything else was circled in black.

Taking their time to divide the room up into different 'search parties', Hadina gave everyone their assignments. By the time they were done, everyone knew what jobs they had to do. Peyton sat with a sad frown on her face, looking at Hadina with those eyes that made her want to cave to Peyton's every whim.

"What?"

"I didn't get an assignment," Peyton whispered back. "I could be useful."

Hadina shook her head and gave Peyton a look that said this

wasn't up for discussion. "You're still healing. You don't need to be out there right now. Trust me. Besides, you'll need to save and compile all your strength for when we get our hands on Demi; you get the honors of annihilating that bitch."

Peyton looked as though she wanted to argue but after glancing at the room around her, she conceded with the dip of her chin.

"Okay!" Hadina barked, clapping her hands together to get everyone's attention. "Y'all have been given your orders. Everyone clear on what they need to do?"

A chorus of yes, boss echoed around the room before she dismissed everyone with a clap of her hands.

The anger in her veins that she tried so hard to dampen down was slowly coming to the surface. Every time they planned their next steps, Hadina was reminded of why they were doing this, how badly Demi had hurt Peyton, and it made her fury rise. She needed her team to act fast because she wouldn't be able to keep it contained otherwise.

Hadina was ready to burn the world down around her, if only to make sure there was nobody left to hurt Peyton ever again.

"Take a breath, baby," came a soft voice from her side. Just the sound of it made her body relax, the tension slowly seeping from her shoulders.

She felt Peyton's arms slide around her waist, her face pressing gently against Hadina's back. It was amazing, Hadina thought, just how much her body reacted to Peyton. Nobody had ever had that effect on her before, and she knew nobody else ever would.

Peyton was *hers*, and she was Peyton's. Their crazies called to each other, their hearts destined to entwine. Hadina didn't believe in fate, but she knew that Peyton was a gift from a higher power.

She allowed herself to stand in Peyton's embrace for a few moments until all the tension had left her. Everyone had left the room, off to start working on their assignments otherwise they'd have to face Hadina's wrath. Which meant, thankfully, both of them were alone. Hadina spun around, leaning the back of her thighs against the table, and pulled Peyton into her.

"Better?" Peyton asked.

Hadina hummed, pressing her face into the crook of Peyton's neck. She always smelt so sweet and Hadina forever wanted to be in her embrace.

"It's always better when we're together."

Peyton leaned back, her blonde hair tickling Hadina's cheek. "What do we do next?"

Groaning, Hadina pouted petulantly. "*Mierda*, I hate that these words are even going to come out of my mouth but...Zellie needs to help you train. She was right, in her own bitch way—I won't be as tough on you because I love you. But we need you to be fully prepared for anything."

"Then let's do it. Plus," Peyton said with a sly grin, "It'll be extra fun for you when I'm a pro and you get to see me kick Zellie's ass."

Hadina barked out a laugh, grabbing Peyton's waist to bring her into a kiss. She was beyond lucky to have found someone like Peyton, and she never wanted to take that for granted ever again.

CHAPTER 20

IT WASN'T LIKE SHE HADN'T TRAINED BEFORE. HADINA HAD BEEN RIGOROUS in initially showing her how to defend herself, and attack if needed. But, well, training with Zellie was a whole different thing.

"Keep your hands up unless you want me to ruin that pretty face," Zellie scolded, motioning to Peyton to bring her arms up higher.

"I'm trying!" she yelled back, throwing a punch that Zellie dodged with ease.

"Barely," Zellie muttered in a low, dull tone.

Peyton circled Zellie on the padded floor, eyes trained on the miniscule movements being made. She needed to figure out Zellie's tell; Hadina told her that *everyone* had a tell, no matter how subtle, and that it was the key to winning a fight. But Zellie was a seasoned fighter and she kept her cards close to her chest.

Managing to get a few steps closer, Peyton hit out with a closed fist, wincing as it connected with Zellie's shoulder when she moved out of the way.

"¡*Patética!*"

Zellie kicked out her foot, sweeping Peyton onto her back. She winced at the impact, anger sparking at her fingertips as Zellie looked down at her with a prideful smirk.

Using her anger to drive her, Peyton smirked, kicking her own legs out. She hit Zellie's ankles hard, bringing the Adis women to the ground. Zellie cursed as she slammed onto her front, sticking her hands out to break her fall.

She made to move but Zellie was quicker, grabbing her by the hair and pinning her down. "Never wear your hair in something so easy to grab. Braid it, put it in a ponytail that's further down your head, or a bun that you can pull out easily. But having your hair on top of your head like this makes you a target. You're easy to take down."

Peyton nodded against her hold, grinding her teeth as Zellie yanked on her ponytail once before letting go.

Her breath was coming in short, stunted waves. Her sides ached and she longed for a break, some cold water, and the soothing touch of her beloved. Instead, Peyton watched as Zellie geared up for round two...or perhaps three—she'd lost count of how many times she'd be thrown onto her ass.

"You're unhealthy."

"I'm not a pro fighter like y'all," Peyton countered with a scowl. "And I'm still healing."

Zellie scoffed. "Nonsense. Healing should give you the motivation you need to be *better*. Stronger. You should be working out every day, making your body a machine."

"The doctor told me to take it easy. To rest until I was healed."

"Pffft. If we all listened to that advice, Adis & Co. wouldn't exist. Sometimes you have to fight through the pain."

"I'm trying, Zellie."

"Not hard enough."

She felt, rather than heard, Hadina come up behind her. The presence of her woman made Peyton stand a little taller, a little more confident. "Stop being so hard on her, Zelina."

Zellie hissed through her teeth. "No. She needs the discipline of someone who isn't holding her hand. *Papi* didn't take it easy on us, Hadina."

Hadina stepped forward, pushing Peyton behind her slightly. Zellie turned around, storming over to the table where her water bottle lay. She took a swig, not bothering to look at them as she spoke.

"You're too soft. She needs to learn the difficult way."

"I think she already learned *the difficult way* when Demi had her held fucking captive, Zellie. Your methods are too rough. Can you stop being a bitch, just for once?"

Zellie spun around, glaring at Hadina. She balled her fists at her sides. "Are you fucking kidding me? I'm not doing this to be a bitch. I'm doing it because I *care* and I want to help! Someone needs to teach her properly. All you do is coddle her like you coddled those fucking tequila bottles when she was missing."

Peyton tensed beside Hadina. "What did you just say?"

"How fucking dare you?!" Hadina screamed. "*¡Mantén tu boca cerrada!*"

In a matter of seconds, something flew through the air towards Zellie. It took Peyton a moment before she registered that it was a knife—and that it was not going in the direction Hadina had intended it to.

Zellie laughed darkly as the knife embedded itself into the wall, nowhere near her. It was obvious from the look on Hadina's face that she'd intended to hurt Zellie, and that she was furious that she hadn't.

Peyton looked down and saw Hadina's hand trembling. As if

sensing her gaze, Hadina looked down too, a pained expression visible on her face.

"Peyton, I-"

Holding up her hand to stop Hadina from saying anything else, Peyton shook her head. "No. I don't want to hear it right now. We'll talk at home."

She made her way over to Zellie, holding out her hand. Zellie waited before finally clasping hands with her.

"Thank you. You're right—I do need your style of training. Give me a day or two, and then we can try again?"

Zellie pursed her lips, nodded, and exhaled slowly. "You're welcome. And I can make that work."

Peyton nodded back and then made her way back over to Hadina. She schooled her face, not allowing Hadina to see the hurt and worry she felt inside, and held out her hand.

Peyton saw the fear behind Hadina's eyes as she linked hands with her.

"Let's go home. We need to talk so we can deal with this together."

***

THE DRIVE HOME WAS SILENT AND FILLED WITH UNEASE. PEYTON WANTED to say something to ease the anxiety that was clearly plaguing Hadina's mind, but she knew that it wouldn't help. Nothing would make either of them feel better until they'd talked, until everything was laid out on the table so that they could work through whatever was happening.

Peyton noted that the leaves on the trees had shifted colors again, some falling down and crunching beneath the tires as they pulled up in front of the house. Don's car was gone, so the house was empty and quiet, perfect for the conversation they were about to have.

"Should I make some coffee?" Peyton asked, her voice surprisingly steady for how uneasy she felt.

"Yes, please. I could do with the caffeine."

Hadina went to the living room and slumped onto one of the sofas. She was slouched, her eyes closed and her head resting back, when Peyton walked in with a mug of coffee in each hand. Hadina attempted a smile in thanks as she accepted the mug, sighing as she took her first gulp. Peyton wanted to wince, knowing how hot it would be, but Hadina was a sucker for self punishment. Scolding her throat with coffee wasn't much different.

Setting her own cup on the table, Peyton took a seat on the sofa beside Hadina. She was tempted to hold out her hand to clasp Hadina's, but settled for folding them into her lap.

"So." she started, "I think you have some stuff to tell me."

Hadina sighed. "Talking about it feels wrong. Like I'm giving it power."

"Baby, it—whatever it is—already has power over you. First, Adrian made a comment about your shaky hands. Now Zellie quips that you were coddling tequila bottles. I've noticed your nightly cold sweats that come with no fever; I should have said something sooner. If this is what I think it is, I *need* you to tell me. And I think you need to voice it to me, so that we can tackle it together."

Hadina's dark eyes filled with tears and she looked away, avoiding Peyton's gaze. She stared out the window, watching as birds built a nest in the branches.

"Losing you was the most difficult thing I've ever been through," Hadina whispered. "And yeah, that seems fucked up to say because I lost *Mama*. But after we lost her, I condemned myself to never dealing whole again. And then I met you, and you took over my heart. And then I lost you, too."

Her voice cracked and Peyton's heart tugged at the pain there.

"I was so *angry*. I had let you run off and I didn't immediately chase you. All I could think about was that whatever was happening to you was all my fault. Meeting me ruined your life, and I didn't know where you were to save you."

Even though Hadina wasn't looking at her, Peyton nodded. She wanted to speak, but Hadina had to take the lead in this conversation.

"Everything hurt and the anger in my veins was so blinding, Peyton. It was taking over me and the more we searched for you and came up empty, the hotter that anger became. I would have destroyed everything if it meant finding my way to you."

Hadina sniffed, swiping a finger underneath her eyes to catch the first of her falling tears.

"I wanted to stop feeling. To be numb. I started drinking, and I guess I didn't stop. The longer you were apart from me, the more I drank. I cooped myself up in the office with tequila bottles and I tried to drown my feelings. The more it burned my throat and made me feel sick, the more content I felt because it was a punishment I deserved."

"*Oh, Hadi*," Peyton whispered quietly, reaching her hand out to gently brush Hadina's shoulder.

Hadina turned to look at her, mascara smearing as tears made a path down her cheeks.

"I was a mess. I wasn't me anymore, and I didn't care. Because it wasn't worth living, or being me, if you weren't by my side. It was easier to numb the pain at the bottom of a liquor bottle than it was to admit that I'd lost you and I couldn't get you back."

Peyton swallowed back her tears. Hadina was always strong for her, so now it was her turn to repay the favor.

"But you got me back, baby."

Hadina shook her head. "But it wasn't easy. I was crazy, Peyton. I was drinking so much that the anger stopped numbing me and just fuelled the fire instead. I yelled at Piper, at Adrian. I stopped eating. I barely spoke to anybody. The days started to blend together and I drank myself into oblivion, because the only time I got to see you was in my nightmares."

She gulped down her coffee and Peyton noted the tremor in her hand, piecing everything together.

"So, what happened? Something had to have changed."

Hadina smirked, though there was no trace of humor in it. "Zelina."

"I'm sorry, *what?* Zellie helped you?"

"I told you, she surprised me too." Hadina sighed. "I showed up drunk at her house. To be honest, I thought she'd leave me in the gutter. But she invited me in, listened to my anger and my accusations. Hell, she let me beat the shit out of her."

"She let you hit her?"

Hadina nodded. "She knew I needed an escape. I had to let the anger out and drinking wasn't doing that for me anymore. I exploded and she let me. And then..."

Peyton tilted her head, wondering why Hadina was so nervous to continue.

"And then she held me as I sobbed. You want to know what changed? Zellie became the big sister I always needed her to be. She helped me fight my emotions, and then vowed to help me find you."

"Wow," Peyton said quietly. "I was not expecting that."

Hadina laughed. "I wasn't either. But it worked. She had connections that I didn't, and she helped me find you."

"And the drinking?"

"I stopped—cold turkey. Terrible idea, in retrospect. I was so unwell with withdrawals, and I won't lie and say that I'm still not tempted to pick up a bottle." Hadina rubbed her forehead, her face contorted in pain. "I get these awful headaches, and sometimes my body aches. Most people become alcoholics over a long period of time, but I did it within weeks. I consumed so much liquor that I'm surprised my body didn't completely shut down on me."

Peyton shuffled forward, taking Hadina's hands in her own, squeezing gently.

"The impact it's had on my body... I'm not in my best form. My aim is off, and I get the tremors in my hands and arms every so often. I'm taking a bunch of vitamins to help strengthen whatever I've damaged inside my body, but I have a long way to go."

"I'm sorry," Peyton whispered, pressing her forehead against Hadina's. "I'm sorry for leaving you, and I'm sorry you had to go through that on your own."

"*Tentadora,* none of this is your fault. I made unhealthy decisions and that's on me. But I found you and I won't let you go again. Though, *I* am the one who's sorry. I know I'm a mess and I hate that this is who you came home to. I'm ashamed and I promise to keep trying until I'm the best version of myself."

Peyton shook her head, sniffling as her own tears mixed with Hadina's.

"I will love you no matter what version of you I get. None of us are perfect, Hadina, and *that* is why we work. We're both fucked up in our own ways, with a truckload of trauma. But we'll get through it all—together."

Hadina nodded, a strangled sob escaping as she leaned into Peyton. They wrapped their arms around each other, feeling their thudding heartbeats between them.

"We will get better, together. When your aim is off, I will be beside you to shoot. When your hands tremble, I will be there to hold them until they still. When your body aches, I will help ease it however I can." Peyton pulled back slightly, holding Hadina's face between her hands. She swiped away the tears, pressing a soft kiss to Hadina's forehead. "And when your heart is heavy and your mind is cruel, making you want to give in, I will hold you and remind you how strong you are. And I will tell you over and over just how much I love you.

"Every version of you is a version I get to love, Hadina. Never apologize for that. The only thing I need is a promise that no matter what happens, we fight and get through it together."

"*Te prometo que.* I promise, Peyton. *Juntos.*"

They stayed like that, huddled together on the sofa, for hours. Peyton held Hadina as she released her tears and her pain, bringing them closer together.

Love was stronger than anything either of them would ever face, and there was no denying the love between them.

That was a bond that would never be broken.

CHAPTER 21

TELLING PEYTON HER TRUTH—EVERYTHING SHE'D BEEN THROUGH AND done to herself while Peyton was missing—had helped Hadina in a profound way. Somehow saying the words aloud had helped her take the first real step in healing. Peyton knew who she was, what she'd done, and she was *still* choosing to stay by Hadina's side.

Hadina didn't deserve her.

But she would keep trying so that maybe one day, she would.

They'd fallen asleep, fully dressed and all talked out, on Hadina's bed around midnight. Now, the sun was shining through the curtains blindingly, and Hadina threw her arm across her eyes.

She groaned, smirking as Peyton stirred beside her and laughed at her dramatics.

"You really are not a morning person, huh?"

Hadina rolled over, nuzzling herself into Peyton's neck, drowning out the light by using Peyton's hair as coverage. "I can be a morning person when I *need* to be. But when I have the opportunity to lay in bed, be lazy, and caress the woman I love...I'll curse the morning sun for ever showing its face."

Peyton chuckled, batting Hadina's hands away as she tickled her sides.

Hadina pressed her lips into the small of Peyton's neck, pressing soft, chaste kisses there. Her touch tickled Peyton, making her wriggle under Hadina's touch.

She let her hands roam, slipping her fingers underneath Peyton's shirt. Her fingertips traced the softness of Peyton's stomach, slowly making their way lower. She was just about to slip beneath the waistband of Peyton's panties when Hadina heard her phone ring, vibrating off the side table.

"*Pinche puta madre,*" she muttered, growling. Peyton laughed as Hadina dramatically threw the covers off her, rolling over to answer the call.

"WHAT?" Hadina barked into the receiver.

Adrian Harris' voice was gruff in her ear. "Good morning to you too, sunshine. I thought you'd like to know that we've eliminated almost everyone on the list. I'm on my way to get Eddie Poplar."

"It's only been a few days," Hadina replied. "You sure Demi's started to get the message?"

Harris tutted. "You know she has. I've made sure of it."

"Fine. Text me the address and I'll meet you there."

The line disconnected and Hadina turned to Peyton. She was surprised to see an excited smile on her face. "You heard?"

Peyton nodded. "Every word. One step closer to ending Demi Treyva's reign of terror and torture."

Both women changed their clothes quickly and headed down to the kitchen. Two cups of coffee later, they were in the car and on the way to the abandoned warehouse location that Adrian had text.

Neither of them spoke during the drive, though everything they wanted to say hung in the air. This was a huge step to getting what they wanted, but it didn't make what they were about to do any easier.

Hadina parked the car outside one of the loading docks. The rusting overhead door was rolled slightly, spilling light on the ground beneath. They didn't normally do anything in the daylight but the regular rules were out the window. Hadina wanted to end this—fast.

Using the chain at the side of the door, Hadina pulled until there was enough space for her and Peyton to duck under. Once they were inside, she nodded to her team who stood, weapons at the ready, in various places around the empty room.

In the center, Eddie Poplar was strapped to a chair using zip ties. His face, which Hadina recognized from the photos, was untouched, though there was blood seeped onto his shirt from somewhere. A little stab wound on the torso, if Hadina was to guess.

Adrian stood behind him, hands on Poplar's shoulders and fingers digging in. "Boss, meet Eddie Poplar."

Hadina looked at him for a moment, silent and contemplative. There was fear in his wide eyes, his mouth quivering as he cried silently. Hadina gave him props for not crying out, begging for his life.

She walked forward, her heels clicking and echoing loudly against the concrete flooring. She stopped in front of him, crossing her arms over her chest. Hadina looked down at him, making her face as expressionless as possible.

"Nice to meet you, Mr Poplar. Do you know why you're here?"

The body nodded, sweat trickling down his forehead. "B-b-because I've been selling in your t-t-terrority."

Hadina laughed. "Little boy, I don't sell *anything*. That shit your boss pushes is poison and I would never sell that to anyone."

Poplar shook his head, his breaths coming in panting heaves. "I d-d-don't understand."

"You will." Motioning Peyton forward, Hadina held out her hand. Peyton took it, stepping up beside her. "This is my woman, Peyton. And that piece of shit you work for took her, beat her, almost killed her. And that is the *least* of what she did."

"I didn't have nothing to do with that. I s-swear!"

"No shit!" Hadina scoffed. "You're nothing but one of her little street rats. But you'll be useful to us, anyway."

Turning to Peyton, Hadina moved her dress to the side, grabbing the dagger she had strapped to her thigh. She handed it to her woman, taking satisfaction in the way Peyton's grip on it tightened immediately.

"This can go super easy for you." Peyton flipped the handle of the knife over in her hand. Hadina noticed the dark, menacing lilt to her voice. "Tell us what we want to know, and maybe you'll survive it. But keep your mouth shut, and what we do to you won't be pretty."

She wasn't sure whether Peyton would actually go through with it, but it made Hadina's insides twist in pleasure at the thought of Peyton committing such acts of violence as retribution for what was done to her.

Eddie Poplar dropped his head, sobbing. "What do you want to know? I'll tell you a-anything, I swear!"

Hadina rolled her eyes, her lip curling in disgust at the ease of how quickly he gave in. If one of *her* team was so weak and willing to betray them, she would *want* them to show up dead. The dead didn't speak, and they sure as fuck didn't snitch.

"We want to know where to find Hernandez."

At the mention of his contact's name, Poplar's head shot up. The fear on his face was palpable. "He'll kill me! Ask me for anybody else, I'll give you them. But he's a freaking psycho and he'll kill me."

Adrian rolled his eyes behind Poplar, squeezing his shoulders with more force. "You're not very bright, are you, Eddie? If you *don't* give us Hernandez, you're going to be dead anyway."

He let out a whimper before nodding. "Okay, fine. We meet at 2208 South Livra Boulevard every Thursday at eleven. Usually just a drop off, but he's always there before we turn up, and he makes us leave first."

Peyton nodded at Harris, who let go of Poplar's shoulders. "And manpower? Is he alone or does he usually bring a team?"

Eddie Poplar slunk back in the chair, looking from Hadina to Peyton. He was weighing up his options, but quickly came to the conclusion that he wasn't escaping this.

"Usually alone. Sometimes he'll bring someone but it's rare. He always has a gun holstered at his waist and on show, but I don't know if he's packing anything else."

"Thank you for your honesty," Hadina stated. "Now that we have that covered, it's time for you to pay for some of the damage you've caused."

The young man's eyes widened and he began thrashing in his chair. "No! No! I didn't do shit. I told you what you wanted to know!"

Peyton rolled her eyes, looking at Hadina for a second before she swung the knife in an arc, creating a gash in Poplar's bicep. Hadina's core constricted as she watched the bloodlust come to the forefront of Peyton's mind, albeit temporarily.

"You're a stupid motherfucker," Peyton snapped. "Everything you do—selling on the streets, or luring young kids away, or even keeping quiet when you know your boss is doing some dodgy shit— impacts on other people. And *everything* your boss stands for is evilness, cruelty, and vileness. You, Mr Eddie Poplar, are directly responsible. Because you do the shit you're told and you don't think twice."

Poplar screamed, sobbing and looking at the blood trailing down his arm.

"Hadina, I'm ready to leave now."

Hadina didn't say anything, simply slid her hand into Peyton's and led them both back to the car. Adrian followed them out, wiping his bloodied hand on a rag.

"Damn, Pey, you're feisty when you want to be. You kicked ass back there." He held up his hand and Peyton high-fived him, making Hadina smirk.

"You know what you have to do?" Hadina asked Harris, leveling her gaze at him. It always amused her when she got to be stern with him. "Don't want you to fuck this up for us."

Adrian flipped her off. "Poplar is going to rest easy here. Ume said she wanted to introduce herself so he'll be well taken care of. I'll make sure to put a first aid kit or two on the table. And while she does that, I'm gathering a few of the team and we'll plan out our little rendezvous with Hernandez."

Hadina nodded once. She didn't always need to use words with Harris, and most of the time he knew what he had to do anyway. They'd worked together for so long, and had been family long before that. He was the best of Adis & Co., though she would never say that to his face.

"Can we go now?" Peyton asked.

"Of course, *tentadora*." Hadina unlocked the car and watched Peyton slide into the passenger seat. She was about to get in the car herself when a thought popped into her head. She turned back to Adrian. "Check in with Piper, okay?"

A worried look flashed across his face and it was the confirmation Hadina needed. "Why? Is she okay?"

"She's fine," Hadina said, a smirk pulling at her lips. "But something tells me she'd be happy to hear from you and know you're okay."

Adrian ran his hands through the thick mess of dark hair atop his head. "Don't meddle, Hadi."

"Me? I would never." She winked at him, seeing the small blush forming on his cheeks. "You both deserve to be happy. But never hurt her or I will personally gut you like a fish, brother or no brother."

He pressed a hand to his heart, feigning emotion. "Oh my, Hadina, I had no idea you thought so highly of me. Should I start calling you sister now?"

"Sure. But I won't be responsible for the knife that ultimately lodges in your throat."

Harris laughed and turned his back, walking into the warehouse.

It was funny that for most of her life, Hadina had known Adrian Harris, had seen him like a brother, but had never said the words. Sure, she'd implied it, but admitting something like that was always a weakness in her eyes. But now, Peyton had widened her heart and broadened her emotional scale. Perhaps it was time she started showing those she loved just how much they meant to her.

Hopping into the driver's seat, Hadina immediately pulled Peyton in for a deep kiss. Her lips still tingled every time and it was a feeling she hoped would last forever.

"What was that for?"

"It wasn't for anything. It's because I love you, and I would never pry my lips away from yours if I didn't have to."

Peyton blushed, tucking a strand of her golden hair behind her ear. "I love you, Hadina."

Hadina grinned, something she only ever seemed capable of doing around Peyton. "Where to now?"

There was a rhythmic tapping for a few seconds as Peyton strummed her fingers off the dashboard while she thought. "Take me somewhere I've never been before."

A sultry, twisted thought arose in Hadina. She laughed, her body fizzling with anticipation.

"I think I have the perfect place."

CHAPTER 22

COMING TO TERMS WITH THE FACT YOU WERE A DIFFERENT PERSON WAS something Peyton had never thought she'd have to do, but life had thrown so many curveballs at her that she no longer had a choice. In the years since Melina had died, she had been through so much and had become someone her sister wouldn't recognize. But, Peyton bargained with herself, she knew her sister would be proud that she had survived and was willing to do whatever it took to stay alive.

But facing Eddie Poplar, thinking about how close they were to getting Demi...It had sent Peyton's anxiety into overdrive. She needed a break from thinking about it, from knowing what was about to come.

"Where are we going?"

Hadina smirked. "Someplace you've never been."

"Tell meeeee," Peyton begged.

"Nope. It's a surprise."

Peyton sat on the edge of her seat with eagerness, watching the city through the window as they drove downtown. So many of the buildings were historical, beautiful looking, resembling old saloons and hideouts.

Hadina pulled over into a parking lot in the middle of town, a bunch of high rise buildings around them, throwing Peyton off the scent.

"Where are we?"

Hadina shook her head, tutting. She went into the trunk of her car, taking out a long piece of black material.

A blindfold.

"What are you up to?"

"Keeping your mind busy," Hadina stated, walking behind her. She gently tied the blindfold over her eyes. She checked that Peyton couldn't see anything—she couldn't—before pressing a soft kiss to Peyton's lips.

Peyton reached out to pull Hadina back to her, but Hadina laughed and stepped out of reach.

"Take my hand," Hadina commanded, entwining their fingers.

Peyton's heartbeat increased as they began to walk. She trusted Hadina and followed her lead, doing what she was told whenever Hadina instructed her to take a step. Before she knew it, Hadina pulled her hand free and told Peyton to stay where she was.

"Hadina! You can't leave me here."

Hadina laughed. "Relax, baby. I'll only be a few steps away."

Peyton stood, waiting rather impatiently, on the spot where Hadina left her. She could hear the passing of keys and Hadina's low murmur of thanks. Her leg shook nervously—with a hint of eagerness—and she struggled against the temptation to remove the blindfold to see where they were.

"Guess who," whispered Hadina's voice, her lips pressed into the shell of Peyton's ear.

A wide grin spread across Peyton's face as Hadina led her by the hand again, guiding her forward. The warm, humid heat of Texas was quickly swept away as they stepped inside a building, the AC brushing their skin with a coolness that made Peyton sigh in relief.

The smell of popcorn filled the air as they headed deeper inside. Once they reached a stop, Peyton gripped Hadina's hand tighter. "Can I take this blindfold off now?"

"*Mi reina, tenga paciencia!* We're going in an elevator and then you'll be able to take it off."

Peyton sighed dramatically, earning an amused laugh from Hadina.

The ping of the elevator door sounded and Peyton was dragged inside the elevator. She tapped her heel against the floor, impatience and adrenaline rising.

It felt like forever before they reached the top, the soft music playing in the background finally stopping.

The smell of food wafted through the air, making Peyton's stomach grumble in response. She was hungry, but also way too excited to be able to eat.

She was relishing in this—time for just her and Hadina, ignoring the rest of the world and pretending like their problems weren't happening.

"Okay, stop there," Hadina commanded, letting go of her hand. "You can take off the blindfold now."

With eager hands, Peyton tore the blindfold off, a gasp escaping her lips once she could see.

They were standing in the middle of the Tower of America, on the very top floor. Even from where they stood, Peyton could see the skyline surrounding them, visible through the large balcony windows.

"This is fucking *beautiful!*"

Hadina grinned, slipping an arm around Peyton's waist and

bringing her closer. "A beautiful place for the most beautiful woman."

Peyton rolled her eyes. "Hardly. But thank you."

Hadina *tsk*'d, shaking her head. She brought her hand to Peyton's cheek, cupping her gently. "I won't have that. You *are* beautiful and that is a fact. You made me feel so much the first time I laid my eyes on you, and that's saying something."

"You know, I used to call you Ice Queen in my head after we first met. You seemed so cold, so sharp, that the name just stuck. But I think I was wrong. I think you're the opposite."

Peyton placed her hand over Hadina's beating heart. "You have this blazing fire roaring through you, bleeding through your veins and begging for release. And to curb it, you put on this front. But then you had to go and choose me, Hadi, to be the one to unleash you. You let yourself feel, let the fire go. I needed you to, and you did. I was burning, and you let yourself burn with me."

Tears pricked at Hadina's eyes and Peyton pressed a soft kiss to her lips. "*Thank you*, Hadina. Thank you for making me feel more beautiful than I deserve, and thank you for giving me the pieces of yourself that you had locked away for so long."

Hadina deepened the kiss, gripping Peyton's waist tightly. When she pulled away, she had left Peyton panting.

"I would do anything for you, Peyton Dimitra. And I'll spend my life showing you that your beauty is immeasurable, your kindness is indescribable, and that your heart is the most precious thing I could ever covet."

They embraced again, this time with more passion and lust behind every move. Peyton craved to be owned by Hadina's touch, her mouth, her love.

"Let's go," Hadina said, breaking the kiss with a sigh. "I have something planned."

Peyton narrowed her eyes but plodded along behind Hadina, following her to the edge of the room.

"Stand right...here." Hadina placed Peyton on the correct spot and then stood beside her. "This room spins, so that you can see the entire city from above. Isn't it glorious?"

Words were lost on Peyton as they took in the sights. It was perhaps one of the most extraordinary things she had ever seen or done. Standing with her love, looking out across the city they called home. It made chills travel up her spine.

A young waiter guided them to a table on the revolving floor, seating them and immediately pouring them glasses of ice water.

"How did you do this?" Peyton whispered incredulously.

"I know some important people. And giving them a little extra money didn't hurt."

For hours, they sat at that table and just talked. Peyton knew it was a way for them to pretend they lived a normal life, doing regular jobs and being happy with the mundane. It was a fantasy they'd give into, just this once, but it wouldn't last. They were not the kind of people to thrive under the regular circumstances everyone else did; Peyton knew that now.

"Are you ready for the next surprise?" Hadina asked, a sly smile on her face.

"This wasn't the main surprise?"

Hadina shook her head. "Not even close."

Reaching into her pocket, Peyton watched as Hadina brought out the blindfold she'd discarded earlier. She didn't dispute it as Hadina stood behind her, carefully tying the material over her eyes again, her fingertips trailing down Peyton's arms.

The whoosh of a door opening made Peyton's knees weak, knowing that it was the balcony door as the noise of the city below filled the air around them.

"Hadina..."

"Trust, remember? I've got you. I'll keep you safe."

A horrible part of Peyton wanted to reply: *What happened to keeping me safe when I was taken?* But she knew that was an ugly, bitter part of herself that she would have to keep combatting. She had forgiven Hadina, but it didn't make it easy to forget.

Shoving the snarky response down, she nodded and allowed Hadina to guide her. She knew from the step down and the way the air hit her that they were officially outside, standing on the balcony. Just the thought made Peyton's knees wobble.

The wind wrapped around them, pushing Peyton back against the windows. She let go of Hadina's hands and pressed her palms against the cool glass.

"Hadi, what's happening?" Peyton's voice drifted, sounding garbled through a gust of wind.

"Shhh, no talking," Hadina whispered in her ear. "It's time to just *feel*."

To prevent her from responding, Hadina kissed Peyton. It was a slow, burning kiss that made every part of Peyton's skin come alive. Hadina pushed herself against Peyton, her fingertips tracing down her arms and to her hips, where she held tightly.

Peyton couldn't bring herself to move her hands from the glass. She was only too happy for Hadina to lead. Her skin felt hot and sweaty despite the cold air whipping at her. Every kiss and touch of Hadina's soft lips made her feel like she was on fire.

"Oh, *fuck*," Peyton sputtered as Hadina slid her hand beneath the waistband of Peyton's pants. Was this really happening? Having sex at the top of the Tower of Americas—on the balcony no less—was like a weird sort of fever dream, filled with fear and anticipation.

Hadina's fingers teased at her through the thin cotton of her panties. She was wet already from the thrill of exhilaration, ready for more. Her mouth opened on a silent gasp as Hadina deftly moved the material to one side and began to toy with her, rubbing and tugging at her clit.

She wanted to beg for more, but Hadina was already a step ahead of her. A single finger slipped inside her, curling to elicit pleasure from her. Peyton's breaths grew heavy, her chest rising and falling as she sucked in air.

The pressure built inside her, making her legs clench together. Desperation for release clung to her, but Hadina knew her body, and right as she was about to reach her climax, Hadi removed her fingers. Peyton was about to protest but Hadina crushes their lips together, her tongue prying open Peyton's mouth. They moaned simultaneously, Peyton delighting in their embrace.

She was getting used to the back-and-forth of their mouths, the air between them short gasps when their kisses had gone on for too long, when Hadina's hand returned to her pussy. Peyton groaned when Hadina wet her fingers using Peyton's slickness, before pushing into her again.

Hadina's pointed fingernails created a sharp sting inside her as she curled her fingers, hitting Peyton's G-spot in the process. It was Peyton's favorite kind of sex with Hadina; a little bit of pain mixed with her pleasure. She knew that Hadina knew that too.

"That's it, baby," Hadina cooed, working her fingers.

Peyton began to move her hips, riding on Hadina's fingers to get more friction, more pressure. Hadina pressed harder into Peyton, moving her hand faster, her thumb entering the equation as she started to tease and flick her clit.

Hadina's breath was hot against Peyton's neck as she bit down, her tongue licking over the teeth marks.

"Take your blindfold off for me, *tentadora.*"

Her hands shook as Peyton did as instructed, removing the blindfold. She gulped in air when her eyes finally adjusted, seeing the San Antonio skyline for the first time in person. It was beautiful, with all its twinkling lights and different types of buildings. The *whoosh* of cars driving way below was carried by the wind, whispering in her ears.

"Oh, *oh, yes,*" she panted, her hands now firmly gripping Hadina's shoulders.

"Look down, love. See how high you are, how high you can soar."

Peyton nodded—her legs like jello, supported by Hadina's hold on her—and gazed below. Adrenaline filled her, her stomach filling with butterflies. Her body shuddered, her climax taking hold. She moaned, yelling Hadina's name, as she let herself go. She fell over the edge of pleasure, a heady and terrifying feeling since there was a very prominent, deadly edge she could really fall over.

The danger mixed with her pleasure and Peyton felt every aspect of her body light up at the feeling.

By the time she had come down, Hadina was standing beside her, hand in hers, grinning that devilish grin.

"That was..."

"Incredible," Hadina finished, licking her lips. "And just a taste of all the things I want to make you feel. Forever."

Peyton's breath caught in the back of her throat and she found herself at a loss for words. The forever Hadina promised was the thing she wanted most in life, and that scared her.

Both women looked out towards the city, their home. They had trouble coming their way, but Peyton and Hadina were strong enough to get through it. Once Demi was out of the picture, they could start living their forever.

"To building the forever life we crave," Peyton said, before pulling Hadina into a kiss that she hoped was filled with every feeling she had. From the way Hadina responded, she knew it did.

CHAPTER 23

THE SCREAMS OF DERICK HERNANDEZ WAS LIKE A SYMPHONY PLAYING IN Hadina's ears. She never got tired of hearing the tortured screams of the scum they captured. Especially when they belonged to someone who had hurt her *tentadora*.

"Tell us where Demi is, *eres una vasca*."

Hadina's knife plunged into the man's gut, pushing through the resistance of layers of skin until she couldn't force the blade further.

"I already fucking told you; I'm not a rat! I'm not going to tell you anything, *pinche puta!*"

Adrian chuckled from beside Hadina, his tattooed arms exposed and crossed over his chest. "That's a decision you should really reconsider, buddy."

"*Chingas tu madre!*"

"Suit yourself," Hadina said with a shrug, before twisting her knife. "You're not needed while you're alive."

The thing about fear was that it wasn't escapable, not for anyone. Talking a big game or acting fearless didn't mean that terror wouldn't reach your heart at some point. Hadina had seen it happy to so many people, and she was watching it happen to Derick Hernandez.

His eyes widened slowly, realization setting in. Hadina didn't much care whether he was scared or not; she'd given him an opportunity to talk and he'd refused. What happened next was solely on him.

Hadina pulled her knife free, holding it up in front of Hernandez, before she swung it down on his hand. It wasn't the first time she'd done it, so she knew the amount of force needed to do what she wanted. A smile crept on her face as two of his fingers on his right hand severed, making Hernandez shriek in agony.

She sidestepped the blood pooling from his hand, nodding to Harris who grabbed a hammer from their tool table beside them.

"Just fucking kill me already!" he screamed.

"That would be too good for you, *cabrón*." Smashing the hammer down, Adrian connected it to Hernandez's kneecap. The sound of bones breaking was unmistakable.

"You know, Derick, I am an artist much like my *hermanita*, Piper," Hadina said. She squatted in front of Hernandez, making sure they were at eye level so he could see the seriousness and darkness in her gaze. "But unlike her, my tool of trade is death. And I am about to paint my masterpiece."

Their back-and-forth method of torture went on for hours until Derick Hernandez was a bruised, bloody, and broken mess. Both Hadina and Adrian Harris were covered in blood splatter, their hands covered and sore.

Hadina wiped her hands on a clean rag, watching as the deep red smeared across her skin. Sometimes she thought that her hands were permanently red, her skin stained and tainted with the amount of blood she'd spilled.

"I'll give you one last chance," Hadina said, throwing the now saturated rag onto the table. She looked at her handiwork on Hernandez's chest: four letters carved into his skin to show Demi Treyva exactly who had done it to him.

ADIS.

"Tell us where your bitch boss is hiding out."

Hernandez groaned, gurgling on his own blood as he opened his mouth. His eyes were practically swollen shut, his lips triple the size and split open in numerous places. Still, the bastard found enough strength to spit at her.

"Go fuck yourself." The words were garbled but Hadina had heard them enough times to know what he was saying.

Hot, red anger flashed behind her eyes. She looked down at her expensive booties, seeing the glob of saliva and blood resting on the toes. Hernandez was lucky he was going to die anyway, because she'd have made him pay for that act alone.

"I have my woman for that. Pity for you that you'll never get to experience that again."

Reaching into her boot, she pulled free the dagger she'd kept hidden. She flipped it over in her hands, reading the inscription. *Sé a la luz.* The dagger that had started so much drama in her life, but had also allowed her to be honest with Peyton. Now she would get to use it to exact revenge for the love of her life.

Moving to stand behind Hernandez, Hadina pressed the blade to the man's throat. She pulled her arm back, curving it around and applying force, feeling the blood pour from the wound.

Hadina stood, waiting patiently for him to die. While she waited, Harris went into the little office behind them, dragging Eddie Poplar out by the hair. They'd tied him to a chair in front of half a dozen monitors, all pointing at different angles of the warehouse. One of the team had stood behind him, forcing him to look ahead and see every single thing that happened to Derick Hernandez. He needed to understand that if that could happen to someone way above him, far worse would happen to him if he didn't comply.

"Thank you for joining us, Mr Poplar. Did you enjoy the show?"

Poplar hung his head low, his shoulders shaking in silent, racking sobs. Adrian grabbed him from beneath the chin, forcing his head up to look at Hadina.

"You've seen what we can do. What we *will* do. You, Eddie, are worthless compared to your comrade. So, I'm sure you can imagine what we'll do to you if you don't do what we ask. Correct?"

He nodded, a slight movement against Harris' tight grip. "I u-unders-s-s-tand."

"I really hope that's true. Because what happens next determines your future."

Clasping her hands behind her back, Hadina began to pace. "We're going to give you a car and the body of your deceased friend here." She nodded to where Hernandez was slumped over in the chair, his blood a pool beneath him. "And you're going to take him directly to Demi Treyva."

"But I don't know where she is!"

Hadina rolled her eyes. "She'll find you, *pendejo*. You think she doesn't know that her entire team has been wiped out? The second she realizes that you're the only one left alive, she'll want to meet you to question you."

"Just kill me! She's going to do it anyway," he sobbed.

Hadina slapped him across the face, hard enough to see the welt forming on his cheek. "You don't get to make requests or tell me what to do. You're right; she will kill you. But if we kill you first, we don't get *her*. And then all of this will have been for nothing. I will get Demi Treyva and if you fuck this up for me, not even death will prevent me from destroying you. I'll make sure that there won't be any sort of afterlife for you. Are we clear?"

Poplar nodded again, his lips pressed in a firm line.

"What are you going to do to her?" he asked sheepishly.

"I'm going to make her feel so empty and worthless that she'll be begging for forgiveness. For mine, for Peyton's, and most importantly, God's. Her maker may forgive her, but that's not up to me. I'm just the one who'll be arranging their meeting."

CHAPTER 24

SITTING AT THE KITCHEN ISLAND, PEYTON RAPPED HER FINGERTIPS ON HER mug of coffee. Hadina had been away for hours already, and she could only assume what she was doing to Derick Hernandez. So, instead of focusing on how scared she was, she was texting back and forth with Kaira. Not that it was helping any.

Kaira: You doing okay?

Peyton: no. Im freaking tf out

Kaira: H knows what she's doing

Peyton: True. But im still getting used to this life. What if shes in danger

Kaira: *eye roll emoji*

Kaira: H can handle herself. And she's got Harris with her

Peyton knew that Kaira was right, but it didn't ease her nerves. It wasn't that she thought Hadina couldn't handle things herself— she most definitely could—but Peyton secretly hated the fact she wasn't with her. That everything was happening because of *her* and instead of being part of the action, she was sitting at home so that she wouldn't be scarred further.

"Honey, I'm home," Hadina called out, the sarcasm dripping in her voice. Such a sweet, gentle greeting and both women knew it didn't fit them or their lifestyle.

Jumping off her stool, Peyton ran to the hallway to see Hadina standing in the foyer, her clothes covered in blood. Even her face was marked with crimson.

"Hadi! Are you okay?" She ran forward, taking Hadina's face in her hands to check for any wounds or signs that she was harmed.

Hadina nodded, taking Peyton's hands and pressing a chaste kiss to them. "I'm okay. It's not my blood."

Peyton blinked. "That's a lot of blood. Tell me it belonged to Hernandez."

"It does." Hadina grinned, all teeth and viciousness. It sent a flutter through Peyton. "We got him... Poplar is on his way with a car and body. Adrian has the tracker, so he'll be trailing him. Shouldn't take long for Demi to realize what's going on."

"So, what now? We just sit around and wait?"

Hadina shrugged off her jacket, revealing an extra bloody shirt. "First, I need to take a shower. And then I have to sleep. What comes next... Well, we'll need all the energy we can get. You should get some sleep too, *tentadora*."

Peyton trailed after Hadina as they made their way to their bedroom—formally Hadina's, but Peyton spent most of her time there now anyway. Slowly, she peeled off Hadina's bloody clothes, depositing them in the laundry basket beside the door. Then she turned on the shower, adjusting the heat until the temperature was perfect.

Taking Hadina by the hand, Peyton led her inside the walk in shower.

"You're still fully clothed."

Peyton tutted, walking into the shower with her, the water

soaking into her clothes. "Wet clothes can be dried. Let me take care of you, baby."

Hadina acquiesced, taking a step backwards to give Peyton more room. While she would never tell Hadina, Peyton had heard her pained cries in the shower after she'd tended to business. This was the only way she knew to make it even slightly better for Hadi, to take away some of the work so she didn't have to think or feel or do anything.

Taking the bottle of body wash from the shelf, Peyton lathered up her hands and began to rub at the red stains covering Hadina's body. Hadina sighed softly, closing her eyes and letting the water cascade down her face. Peyton's touches were gentle and slow. There was something sensual about it, without it being arousing. She wanted to look after Hadina in the way she knew her love would look after her.

With an extra level of delicateness, Peyton washed Hadina until she was clean. Hadina stayed silent, only emitting another sigh when Peyton began to wash her hair. She took extra care with Hadina's long, raven locks as she shampooed and rinsed, repeating the process again. Only when Peyton had applied conditioner and was rinsing it out did she feel Hadina begin to tremble. Her body shook in silent tremors and Peyton felt the hot tears run down Hadina's face.

Grabbing a towel from the rack on the wall, Peyton switched the shower off and wrapped Hadina up. "Let's go, love."

Hadina nodded, letting Peyton lead them to the bed where she pulled back the duvet, ushering Hadina to lay down. Stripping herself of her now wet clothes, Peyton crawled in behind Hadina, curling her body. Entwining themselves together, Peyton held Hadina close until they both drifted off to sleep.

Almost twenty-four hours had passed by since Hadina had sent Eddie Poplar off with a beat up car and the dead body of Derick Hernandez. Peyton had woken up to breakfast tacos and a mug of freshly brewed coffee, courtesy of Hadina. But then the day turned into a waiting game and both of them were starting to get anxious.

"You have no patience," Zellie muttered from where she sat, cross-legged, in the plush emerald armchair.

Peyton scoffed. "People in glass houses shouldn't throw rocks."

"Stones. It's supposed to be stones."

"Urh! Same difference."

Hadina laughed and pressed a soft kiss to the side of Peyton's neck. "I like it when you yell at my sister."

Peyton blushed, burrowing further into Hadina's side.

"*¡Consigue una habitación!*"

Both Peyton and Hadina looked up to glare at Zellie. "You're the one in *our* space."

Zellie flipped them off. "This is a *family* room in our family house. I am allowed to be here."

"Hm, true. But are you wanted here?" Peyton countered, a sudden bout of confidence coming over her.

"Ooooh, so feisty. Hadi, your kitty has claws."

Hadina rolled her eyes, making Peyton laugh. Even if she wasn't Zellie's biggest fan, which seemed like an understatement, Peyton had to admit that she enjoyed seeing some humor between Zellie and Hadina. After all they'd gone through, a bit of hilarity was the least they deserved.

The tune of Hadina's phone loudly interrupted their playful bickering. Peyton sighed, seeing Harris' name on the screen. There was no denying the fact that shit was about to go down.

"*Ta bueno. ¿Qué pasa?*"

Peyton watched Hadina tap the screen to put Adrian on speakerphone, placing the phone between them on the table. Zellie raised her eyebrows, leaning forward in her chair.

"La tenemos. We got her. I was tracking Poplar and he went to one of the regular meeting points. I guess Treyva had anticipated it because she was waiting for him. Then a text came through on the burner phone; an address and time to meet."

Hadina sucked air through her teeth. Zellie grinned ferociously. Peyton, however, watched as her hands began to tremble where they were folded in her lap.

"Tomorrow. Eight p.m. She even signed it as *Regina*."

"Send a text back to confirm."

This was what they'd been waiting on. What Peyton had wanted ever since she got back to the Adis home.

Revenge.

Retribution.

Vengeance for her sister. For herself.

Yet, anxious thoughts still tugged at her. What if they couldn't kill her? She'd been an aloof presence all this time; what was different now?

"You are."

Hadina's voice broke through Peyton's cycle of perturbed thoughts. She hadn't realized that she'd been talking aloud. Even Zellie was looking at her, as though she was trying to give her extra confidence through her gaze alone.

"We've never tried to take her out before. But what's different now is that we have you, *tentadora*. You are stronger than you give yourself credit for, and your mind is an invaluable weapon to Adis & Co."

"She's right," Zellie replied. "Besides, this is the first time in a long time that we are all together. Fighting together. Watching each other's backs. This is one bitch ass woman against the elite Adis family. And that includes you, Peyton."

"You're an Adis now."

CHAPTER 25

Nerves wracked Hadina, making her uncomfortable and almost overwhelmed by the feeling. She was used to high stakes, murder, and the violent tendencies that came with her job—but she wasn't used to the need for revenge for someone she loved. Her love for Peyton was something unlike she'd ever felt, and the vengeance she craved on her behalf was a roaring storm inside her.

There was something about Peyton's gentleness that had slowly seeped into Hadina, stealing her heart in the process. Simple things she did to show affection made Hadina want to melt on the spot. She thought about the night she'd taken Peyton out a cruise, showing her some of the back streets of San Antonio. Hadina had always been partial to fast cars and loved the feeling of being thrown back against the seat, changing gears, and hitting the gas as hard as she could.

While she was driving, Hadina had a tendency to keep her hand on the shifter. It was a small thing that Peyton had apparently picked up on because she placed her palm atop Hadina's, entwining their fingers. Switching gears together, squealing whenever Hadina hit the gas a little harder.

Hadina loved that sound; Peyton screaming in delight at something so innocent. Her squeals turned into excited giggles when Hadina had punched the clutch, putting the car in a rolling burnout before they shot off into the night, down the empty streets. Hadina had caressed her thumb as she drove, thanking God for being blessed enough to have been given Peyton.

Now, her nerves built as her body twitched anxiously. She had let Peyton into her heart completely and now the very idea of losing her made her more nauseous than she thought possible.

Peyton, however, didn't seem nervous at all. Hadina knew she was deep down, but her exterior presented no signs of worry. She just appeared tense, rigid, like she couldn't wait for it all to be over.

Hadina could understand that.

"Is it time yet?"

"Almost."

They were waiting in Hadina's Cadillac, lights off and weapons at the ready. Harris was scoping out the building, knowing that Demi Treyva liked to play dirty. But Hadina was almost sure that the woman was out of tricks to play. This would be their last showdown, the final time they'd ever have to see each other.

One of them wouldn't be walking away, and Hadina knew it wouldn't be her.

Demi Treyva's rule of terror had come to an end. Hadina planned to make it as bloody and brutal as possible.

Hadina's phone vibrated and she saw a text from Harris come through.

Harris: All good, boss. She's alone.

Hadina: Roll in. On our way.

"Ready?"

Peyton looked at her, nodding. "Let's finish this."

Hadina leaned over, grabbing Peyton's face and bringing their lips together in a rushed, heated kiss. "No matter what happens, know that I love you immeasurably."

"And I love you, Hadina."

They got out of the car and made their way inside the building. In one hand, Hadina had her gun in a tight grip, finger pressed to the edge for easy access to the trigger. In the other hand, she was gripping a dagger. She didn't know which method of torture she'd prefer in the moment. Peyton was gripping her favored dagger in her hand, looking deadly and ready for action. If it wasn't such a high stake moment for them, Hadina would have considered pulling her woman off somewhere and making good use of both knives.

"Stay quiet and behind me," Hadina ordered.

"I'll be quiet, but I'm not leaving your side," Peyton countered. It was infuriating to Hadina, but she also loved seeing Peyton not be scared to answer back. She would never have to cower to anyone ever again, if Hadina had anything to do with it.

The meeting point was an old hotel, one that was long since abandoned. Most of it was a crumbling mess, apart from the dining hall. That room had been cleared out and had been frequented by squatters for most of Hadina's life. She assumed that was how Demi had found half of her team—targeting the vulnerable and promising them riches.

Entering the front of the building, both Zellie and Piper joined them, walking at their flanks. Adrian was somewhere, having found the best vantage point for if everything hit the fan. He'd take the kill shot if needed. There was no way Demi Treyva was leaving alive.

As they reached the dining hall, Hadina began to feel the hairs on her arms stand up. There was a change in the atmosphere and she didn't like that; Hadina was one for always trusting her gut.

They pulled the large double doors open, revealing Demi

sitting on a rusting chair, a smug smile on her face. Her short, blonde hair was pulled back behind one ear, and a bright red was painted on her bitter lips.

"So glad you ladies could join us."

Us.

A shiver ran down Hadina's spine and she looked to Peyton, seeing that she was equally as tense. Something was wrong.

Hadina tightened her grip on her weapons, catching Peyton doing the same from the corner of her eye.

A gasp tore free from her as a figure emerged from the darkened doorway behind Demi. Standing tall and stern, Hadina's father stopped beside Demi. The way they were standing...it looked like a united front *against* Adis & Co., the very company he had created.

"*Papi?*" Piper's voice broke through the tense silence, her tone covered in betrayal.

"*¿Qué has hecho?*" Zellie asked, disbelief coating every word.

Hadina stood rigid in her place, just staring at her father. The way it looked, the feeling she had in her gut... She had to be wrong.

"Answer us, *Papi!*" Piper yelled. It was the first time Hadina had ever seen her lose her temper with their father. "Don't just stand there!"

He didn't say a word. His gaze was directed at Peyton, intense and filled with unsaid words. Something about that—the betrayal, the lack of communication—set Hadina on edge and she gritted her teeth. He'd betrayed Peyton once before; Hadina wouldn't let him do it again.

She'd wait until he said his piece. After that, Hadina would ruin Demi, whether her father was in league with her or not.

"Enough of this family bullshit!" Demi yelled, clapping her hands together as she stood up. "I'm so sick of all of you Adis' and your whining and complaining. Does it ever stop?"

Hadina pointed the tip of her knife in Demi's direction. "You, keep your fucking mouth shut." She turned the blade towards her father. "As for you, *Papi*, I think it's time you spoke."

Her father looked at her with heartbroken eyes. "You don't understand, *mija*."

"It isn't the first time you've said that to me, *Papi*. I'm sick of hearing it."

"Oh, boo-freaking-hoo. Big, bad Hadina Adis has had her feelings hurt. I swear, you're all fucking pathetic. You, and your love-stricken ways. So foolish. You love that little bitch so much, but you didn't manage to stop me from taking her, did you?" Demi sneered, looking down her nose at Hadina. "Didn't manage to stop me from breaking her and leaving her a bloody mess either."

Hadina was about to answer her, a slew of vile things on the tip of her tongue, but Peyton grabbed her wrist, shaking her head almost imperceptibly.

"And *you*," Demi said, rounding on Zellie, "what a pussy. You chickened out of our deal, and clearly you've gone soft. I would call you weak, but I don't think that even covers how pathetic you are."

Zellie's nostrils flared and she trembled with rage. But for the first time, Hadina's sister stayed in her place, waiting to be commanded. She had told Hadina that they'd do this her way, and clearly Zellie was determined to keep her word.

"And don't even get me started on you." Demi had turned towards Piper, her eyes assessing. "Clearly the runt of the litter. So unimportant that you don't even get to play with the big girls, huh? You're basically a side note. Tell me, are you even worthy to have the Adis name? You sure as fuck aren't worthy to be in *my* presence."

Tears sprung in Piper's eyes, Demi's cruel words striking deep with some of Piper's deepest insecurities. Hadina was desperate to move, to do something, but if Peyton wanted them to wait, then wait they would.

Demi slowly turned back to Peyton, her smug face lighting up with excitement. "If it isn't my darling daughter! Pity to see you're still alive and in one piece. I did make a mistake—letting those two idiots stay with you while I took care of business. As the saying goes, if you want something done right, do it yourself. So, lucky me! I get to be the one to end your piteous existence."

The foul words coming out of her mouth towards Peyton was Hadina's breaking point. Without thinking, she pulled her arm back and watched as her knife split through the air, embedding in Demi's thigh, a grin pulling the corners of her lips as Demi screamed in pain.

Keeping her voice calm, almost dull, Hadina let the dark part of herself roam free. The lethal demon she kept at bay was now at the forefront, ready to destroy Demi Treyva. "How dare you speak to my wife like that? You're not even worthy of her glance. Hell, you're not worthy of sharing the same bloodline as her."

She took a step forward, eager to slit Demi's throat so she didn't have to hear her speak ill of Peyton one more time, but Don held up his hand to stop any of them from moving. Hadina looked to her father in confusion.

Reaching out for the dagger, Don gripped the handle while moving his other hand to the pressure point on Demi's neck. Hadina watched as he twisted the knife still stuck in her thigh, eliciting another tortured scream from her. With a kick of his foot, he forced Demi onto her knees, yanking the knife free at the same time. Keeping a grip of her neck, her father pressed the sharp tip of the blade to the underside of Demi's chin.

"You're a foolish woman, Demi Treyva. It seems time has done nothing to give you wisdom." Don let out a sigh. "I came here in the hopes you would take my advice and do the right thing by your daughter. It was an old fool's wish, I know, but I had to try. For the sake of my daughter, and yours. But your fate is of your own making, Demi."

Taking a step back, he removed the blade from her jaw, shaking his head slowly. "You should never have spoken about my daughter's wife with such vehemence. Now, you'll face her wrath."

Hadina could feel her jaw slacken with shock. In her gut, she'd wanted to believe that her father hadn't betrayed them again. But to see him defend them, defend Peyton like that...she was thankful beyond words for having been born an Adis with Don as her father.

He walked towards them and stopped, holding the knife out. "This is for you."

Hadina reached out to take it but Peyton shook her head. "He means me."

Her father nodded, extending the handle of the blade to Peyton. She gripped it tight, and Hadina watched her father do the same to the sharp blade. As Peyton went to pull the knife from his hold, her father held tighter.

The edge cut into his hand, blood pooling in the palm of his hand. When he finally let go, his blood dripping onto the floor between them, he looked to Peyton with eyes full of remorse.

"For my part in your suffering, *cariña*, I am truly sorry."

Removing a handkerchief from his suit jacket, he wrapped it around his palm to stem the bleeding.

"Now it's your time for vengeance. Unleash your wrath, Peyton, and let your eyes be the last thing Demi Treyva ever sees."

CHAPTER 26

She forced her hand to stay steady as Don handed her the dagger. She couldn't help but stare at his blood coating the blade, a sacrifice and an apology.

Peyton didn't realize how much anger she had been harboring towards Don, or just how much guilt he himself was keeping locked away. It seemed they had both buried their feelings, hoping that everything would just work out without ever having to speak about it.

She looked at Hadina, shock and awe in her eyes.

"This is your decision, *tentadora*," Hadina said quietly. She moved in front of Peyton, blocking off her view of Demi. "I can do this for you—I would *love* to do it for you. But I think you need this. You need the satisfaction of being the one to take her from this world."

Hadina was right. Peyton knew she *had* to do this. After everything Demi had done to her, everything she had taken away from her, this was Peyton's chance to give herself closure. It wouldn't be pretty, but it would be enough.

"I can do this."

"Of that, I have no doubt. Go get your revenge."

Hadina stepped to the side, revealing Demi crawling on the floor, a smear of blood left in her trail. Hadina's aim must have been pretty good, because it seemed like Demi was losing a *lot* of blood. Though, she supposed, Don twisting the knife would have helped some.

Taking each step carefully and slowly, Peyton prowled towards Demi calmly. With each step, Peyton was reminded why Demi was a devil in disguise.

She pictured Melina, her beautiful sister, and the life that was stolen from her. Peyton had always imagined Melina standing beside her as she got married, the maid of honor that was so truly beautiful and kind, Peyton wouldn't even have minded if she stole the show. Now that she was with Hadina, and marriage was a very real possibility, it hurt all the more to know that Melina would never be there.

Melina had been robbed of a future. One with a happy and healthy relationship, joyful children brightening her life, and a life-time of love and laughter with Peyton.

For Melina, Peyton would kill Demi Treyva.

Turning her head slightly, Peyton caught the eye of both Zellie and Piper. Both women—her new sisters, she realized—tilted their chins at her in encouragement.

When she reached the crawling Demi, she stomped her foot down on her back, causing the woman to scream.

"Get off me, you little fuck!"

Peyton rolled her eyes. "Get up."

Demi shook her head, refusing Peyton's order. "I don't answer to you, bitch. Don't touch me!"

"GET UP!" Peyton screamed, her voice offering no space for debate. It was a command.

Demi looked up at her, eyes glassy and showing the slightest hint of fear. Peyton removed her foot and watched as Demi slowly tried to stand.

"Look how pathetic you are! You call all of us weak, and now look at you!"

Peyton berated her, looking down in disgust. "You're just a coward at heart, aren't you? That's why you go after the vulnerable; you're too much of a pussy yourself to go after anyone else."

Demi glared at her, standing on shaky feet as blood rushed from her leg wound. "Shut your mouth."

Peyton barked out a laugh and turned to Hadina, throwing her the dagger. "Hold this for me, please, baby."

Turning back to Demi, she remembered all the training from both Hadi and Zellie, and threw a punch. Her fist connected with Demi's nose, the force of the hit causing a flood of blood to pour immediately.

Demi fell to the floor, holding her nose in her hand.

"Come on, you coward!" Peyton screamed, grabbing Demi by the hair. "Hit me! Hit me like you did when I was tied up and defenseless!"

"Says the one fighting me while I'm bleeding out!"

"Ha!" Peyton laughed sardonically. "Poor Demi. Pity I don't feel an ounce of sorrow for you."

Dragging her back to the chair, Peyton smacked Demi's face against the armrest, hearing bones crunch. She let her go, watching as Demi fell backwards. Then she landed a blow to her stomach, before kicking where she'd just kicked.

Inflict as much pain as possible, she told herself.

Demi groaned, trying to find purchase to move, but Peyton moved quicker, kicking at her before stomping down on her wounded leg. The resulting screams made Peyton want to smile.

"You know, Melina was the sweetest soul to ever exist." Peyton sighed, feeling the heaviness in her heart. "The fact you took her from the world is a sadness that's impossible to recover from. You stripped me of the first person who made me feel whole. And it meant I was floating through my life as half a person."

"You'll always be half a person," Demi hissed through gritted teeth. "Because you're *nothing* and you know that. Mommy doesn't love you."

Peyton scoffed. "You're not my mom. I don't need a mother. And you're wrong." Peyton took a step backwards, a smile on her face. "I'm not nothing and I'll never be half a person again. I found a family, on my *own*. I made myself the life I wanted and I found the love of my life. I became part of her family, and I know I won't lose them.

"You're a cruel, evil woman, Demi. You don't know what family or love means. But I do. And I will spend the rest of my life being thankful that you never had a part in who I am, or had the chance to poison any piece of me."

Peyton felt Hadina step forward, slipping her hand into hers. "You'll never be without family again."

"You're one of us," Piper seconded.

"You're annoying as hell, but there's something about you. I guess we're all attached at this point," Zellie said, laughing lightly.

Peyton flipped Zellie off, offered Piper a smile, and turned her gaze to Hadina. "I love you."

Hadina gripped her hand tighter. "I love you, *mi tentadora*." She leaned forward, pressing a soft kiss against Peyton's lips. "Finish this, baby. Finish it and then we can live our lives."

As Hadina pulled away, she pressed the dagger into Peyton's hand. They shared a smile, and Peyton felt renewed in her anger and her search for vengeance.

She turned, making her way back to Demi, who cowered under

her. It was amazing how feeble people became when they feared for their life.

"I hope that your place in Hell is filled with every dark thing you've ever done. Your soul is as tainted as you, Demi Treyva. And I hope you rot."

Lunging forward, Peyton drove the dagger into Demi's chest. She twisted the blade, making sure it caught her heart. Pulling the knife back, she repeated the process. Over and over. Until both she and Demi were covered in blood.

But only Peyton was alive, whole, and able to walk away.

With every splatter of Demi's blood on her skin, Peyton was reminded of finding her sister's blood soaked body, renewing her reason for taking Demi's life.

"That was for Melina," Peyton said as she pulled herself off Demi's dead body. "And for me."

CHAPTER 27

Hadina - two weeks later

It was a bizarre thing, watching the woman you loved get the retribution she had seeked for so long. Hadina had been so desperate to step in, take over, make sure that the blood was on *her* hands. But Peyton had said no. And she was right to do so. Ending Demi Treyva had to be done by Peyton; it was a poetic kind of justice. Killed by the child you brought into the world.

Hadina had been sure that Peyton would break after what happened. Not because she was weak, but because it was such an insurmountable amount of emotion that had been built up and released. It would have been natural—even for Hadina. But Peyton had surprised them all.

"Are you sure you're okay?"

Peyton rolled her eyes, pressing her palm against Hadina's cheek gently. "I won't be if you ask me that one more time. Really, Hadi, I'm doing good. Demi got what she deserved. I refuse to harbor guilt or anything else in response to that."

Hadina pressed her lips together in a firm line. "But that was a big thing to go through. I'm worried that you're bottling it all up and then it's going to break you when you explode."

Closing the distance between them, Peyton slipped her arms around Hadina's waist. She tilted her head up, pressing their lips together in a soft kiss. "Nothing will ever break me again. I avenged Melina, and myself. And now we get to plan ahead for *our* future. I am much stronger than before, baby. Believe me."

Hadina nodded. "I believe you. But it doesn't mean I won't worry. It's my duty."

"As my wife?"

She was caught off guard by Peyton's question. She had called Peyton her wife in the heat of the moment, but Hadina had meant it with every fiber of her being. She had thought of Peyton that way for a while, but had never had the guts to say it aloud.

"Yes."

"You meant it? It was just a spur of the moment thing?" Peyton asked sheepishly, a blush spreading across her cheeks.

Hadina raised a brow, looking down at Peyton with a serious expression. "I meant it entirely, *tentadora*. You are my wife, and I am yours. You didn't really think you could escape me so easily? We are bound."

Peyton took a deep, shuddering breath. Hadina watched as her eyes became glassy before tears spilled down her cheeks. "I never want to escape."

Grabbing her by the waist, Hadina brought them crashing into each other. She tilted Peyton's head up by the chin, enveloping her in a deep, sultry kiss. Their breathing became hot, heavy, and Hadina only pulled away when they both needed to come up for air.

"There is no escape for either of us. Not anymore. We belong to each other now."

Peyton smiled, pressing her face into Hadina's chest as she hugged her tight. "I like the sound of that."

They stayed like that for a while, wrapped up in each other. Hadina caressed Peyton, showing her the softness she needed to know that if Peyton ever did need to speak about what happened, she would be comfortable to speak to Hadina about it.

"What happens next?" Peyton asked, sitting up from where they lay atop the bed.

"What do you mean?"

"Since I killed Demi, I haven't known what to do with myself. Your father clearly doesn't need a caregiver."

Hadina tucked a piece of Peyton's fallen hair behind her ear, grinning. "You find your purpose. There will always be a slew of scumbags like Demi Treyva out there. You're part of the Adis & Co. action now—you just have to find your next scumbag to target."

Peyton practically beamed. "That sounds like a good plan. When can we start?"

Hadina nuzzled Peyton's neck, breathing in her scent. "Now, baby. We can start now."

WITH BLOOD SMEARED ACROSS HER FACE, RED-STAINED BLADE IN HAND, Peyton was a terrifying temptress that made Hadina feel weak at the knees. She looked at the bodies around them, each killed by their hands, and smiled. They were a vicious, psychotic brand of chaos, and Hadina loved every part of them.

Once Harris returned, signaling that the girls had made it out safely, Hadina angled her head and raised her eyebrows, telling him to wait outside. He nodded in reply and smirked, knowing just what perversions she was about to take part in. Still, the knowledge of people being able to hear them, well, it made Hadina's toes curl in anticipation.

Without waiting to hear the click of the door, Hadina marched over to her love, shoving her against the wall. Peyton let out a soft *oof* and grinned wildly at Hadina.

"Baby, is now really the time?"

Hadina growled, running her own knife down Peyton's side. "It's always the time when it comes to you, *tentadora*. Seeing the way you slice these bastards up, ending them for hurting the innocent—how could I not want to fuck your brains out?"

Peyton moaned as Hadina pressed her thigh against her core, moving to create a burning friction to set her alight. Hadina wasn't sure which one of them moved first, but suddenly their lips crashed against each other, Peyton prying Hadina's lips apart with her tongue.

As Hadina slipped her hand beneath the skirt of Peyton's dress, her fingers skimming her already dripping pussy through her panties, she couldn't help but grin. Bringing her mouth to Peyton's ear, she bit down lightly on her lobe. "Not so concerned with getting caught now, are you, baby?"

Groaning as Hadina rubbed her clit through the material, Peyton shook her head. "Let them listen. I want all of them to hear how good you fuck me."

That was all Hadina needed to be spurred on in her assault of Peyton's pussy. Pulling the thin material to the side, Hadina thrust a finger inside of her, curling as she pumped. Peyton lifted her right leg and wrapped it around Hadina's waist, allowing her a better angle. Her fingers dug into Hadina's shoulders, gripping on for dear life as she added a second and then a third finger.

It took mere minutes before Peyton was crying out, her juices flooding Hadina's hand. She continued to work Peyton through her orgasm, waiting until she had stopped pulsing before bringing her fingers out and sucking on them.

"You taste so damn good," Hadina moaned, bringing her fingers to Peyton's mouth for her to taste too. She smeared her juices across her lips, suppressing her own urge to groan as Peyton's tongue darted out to lick her lips.

"Look at you, my little *tentadora*, covered in the blood of our victims, with your honey running down your leg."

Peyton hummed, unwrapping her leg from Hadina's waist and pressing a kiss to her lips. Her hand wrapped around Hadina's wrist, bringing her hand up between them. Her eyes glinted with mischief and a promise of fun. "Now, are you ever planning on using this knife or do I have to do it myself?"

Hadina chuckled, licking her lips in anticipation. She used her free hand to grip Peyton by the throat, tilting her chin up to expose her throat. She peppered kisses lightly across the tender skin, before biting down to elicit a whimper from her girl.

"You should know by now that you don't need to do anything by yourself, least of all that."

Peyton was pliant in her hands, though Hadina could feel the way her pulse raced when she tightened her grip. Hadina eyed her dress, noting the way it dipped across her chest, exposing her collarbones and shoulders to the world. It clung to Peyton's curves in all the right places, accentuating her breasts and hips. It drove Hadina fucking wild.

She brought the steel blade up to Peyton's chest, holding the sharp edge against the dip of her collarbone. Adding slight pressure, Hadina made sure Peyton could feel the coolness of the metal against her skin but prevented herself from breaking the skin.

"Please, Hadi," Peyton groaned, "stop teasing."

"I'm the tease?" Hadina questioned, a smug grin on her face. She looked down between them, feeling Peyton's chest heave against her. She could see the swell of her breasts and the slight hint of cleavage, threatening to send Hadina into overdrive. "You've been teasing me all fucking night in this damn dress."

Peyton couldn't help but grin wickedly. "I know you love this dress."

"I love it for my eyes. But all these bastards seeing you look so sinfully hot before you slit their throats? It was almost too much for me to handle."

"Then maybe you should teach me a lesson so I don't do it again, *mi amor*."

Hadina pursed her lips and locked eyes with Peyton as she dug the blade into her skin, pulling it down as she felt blood bloom around the edges. Peyton closed her eyes and pressed her head back against the wall, sighing contently as Hadina marked her skin.

"I haven't been able to stop thinking about cutting you here and running my tongue across that dip," Hadina said, moving her dagger to the other hand so she could run her finger through the blood. "Of tasting your blood and theirs together, relishing in the fact that you were responsible for their deaths."

"So, taste me," Peyton whispered, opening her eyes to look at Hadi. There was nothing but love and desire there, begging for pleasure. Hadina had helped free Peyton from the angelic duties she felt had cursed her, and both of them relished in it. This thing between them—be it love, lust or some crazy brand of obsession— was twisted and dark, but it was theirs.

Leaning forward, Hadina dipped her head to Peyton's chest, running her tongue along the wound. She growled and lapped up the blood trickling from the cut, swirling her tongue to mix the taste of her *tentadora* and those she had so beautifully ended. It sent Hadina into overdrive, her pussy weeping between her thighs.

"Fucking divine."

Peyton hummed and ran her fingers through Hadina's raven hair, tugging slightly in a way she knew made Hadina crazy. Hadi moved in again, making another cut diagonally across the wound to form an X. "So that everyone knows you're taken," she said before closing her lips around the wound and using her tongue to show Peyton just who she belonged to.

While she kissed, licked and bit on the over-sensitive area of Peyton's collarbone, she moved her fingers between her thighs and immediately slipped them inside Peyton, knowing she was ready for her again. They became a collection of moans and groans, each of them getting off by the pleasure of their counterpart. While Hadina wanted nothing more than for Peyton to make her scream too, she didn't need for that to happen for her to feel satisfied. If Peyton was happy and fucked into oblivion, Hadina had found that she was also rather fulfilled.

With one final pump of her fingers, coupled with her teeth grazing the wounds on her chest, Hadina had Peyton crying out, screaming her name as she collapsed against her.

As Hadina removed her fingers and helped Peyton regain her balance, she found herself smirking. "Well, *tentadora*, I think they certainly heard how hard I made you come, don't you think?"

COMING SOON...

Roots of Ruin
Modern Goddess Series
Book Three

SARAH JAMES

Another Note:

The introduction of additional characters—Darío and Itza—were courtesy of the wonderful V. Domino. Her series *An Acapulco Affair* is incredible and we couldn't resist the urge to crossover our characters. If you'd like to read more about Darío and Itza, I strongly encourage you to read *Mi Deseo (My Desire)* by V. Domino. It's wonderfully dark and twisted, just like the Modern Goddess series, with a cartel twist. And keep your eyes out for future projects... There may be more crossovers coming up.

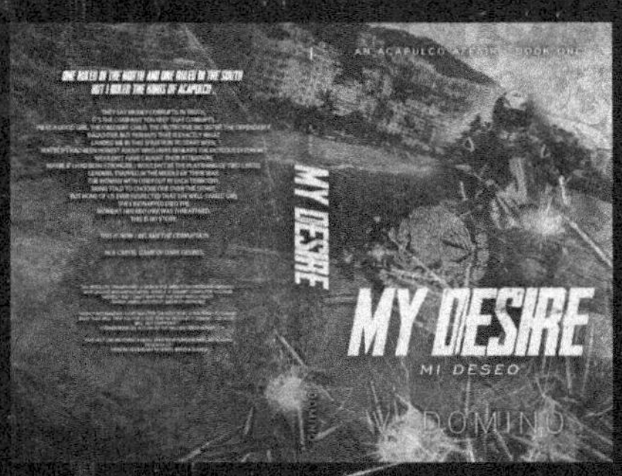

ACKNOWLEDGMENTS

The first thank you belongs to my best friend and incredibly talented fellow author, V. Domino. Baby, you are the most amazing person and best friend I could wish for. This book would literally not have happened without your cheerleading, and sternness when you know I absolutely *had* to be writing but was procrastinating (like I always do). Thank you from the bottom of my heart for the work you've put into BoB by my side, and for sharing more of your culture with me to ensure that the Latinx representation was accurate. None of the Adis sisters would be a fraction of the characters they are without your input. Thank you also for letting me borrow your characters. Darío and Itza were such a fun surprise in this book and I hope we can have more crossovers in the future. I could go on forever, but that would end up the size of the book. *Tu eres mi hermosa estrellas.* I love you and I will be forever grateful for you. Here's to all our future plans.

To Gabe, for always putting up with my endless questions and asking for translations, even when you're busy. Thank you for also providing me with laughter and light when I was stressed by deadlines and needed a break. Love you lots. You're a badass, Peaches!

Eliza, my hype woman and PA. You're an invaluable part of my process, and my life. Thank you for being by my side through everything and for supporting my writing always. The years of friendship with you mean so much to me and I am overjoyed that you're part of this journey with me. I can't wait for all the fun things we get to do together in the future. And yes, you still have dibs on Harris. Love you!

To my street team, thank you for the hype and support! It doesn't go unnoticed and I'm incredibly grateful.

And lastly, my wonderful readers. You have shown so much love to my crazy, morally messed up characters and it means so much to me. Thank you for making my dreams come true.

SARAH JAMES

ABOUT THE AUTHOR

Sarah James is an author of dark and smutty romances. She strongly believes that villains do it best and you'll find her usually rooting for them. When she's not writing, editing or designing covers, she'll be trying to get through some of her never-ending TBR or making pinterest boards for all her different book ideas.

Sarah James is a pen name for author *Colby Bettley*.

You can find up to date information or follow her on social media at: https://linktr.ee/authorsarahjames